ALSO BY LOU IOVINO

Skybound

I0626353

DATA MINE

LOU IOVINO

Copyright © 2022 by Lou Iovino

All rights reserved. Published by LAB Press, LLC, New Jersey.

Cover design by Damonza.

ISBN 978-1-7371746-1-5 (trade paperback)

ISBN 978-1-7371746-3-9 (e-book)

For Jill

"The welfare of humanity is always the alibi of tyrants."

—Albert Camus

CHAPTER
ONE

DATA FLICKERS and flashes over the screens of the array like sunlight on water, a dazzling display filled with wonder and mystery like the life it represents. The volume and variety of information constantly streaming into the system can be overwhelming for even the most seasoned data miners. But Gwen Elliott has always been able to look beyond the sparkling biometric ripples and alphanumeric eddies, to see through even the most turbulent inputs to the dark truths lying beneath the surface. She knows where to cast her line.

"So, what's this one's deal?"

"Mid-forties, married, one kid," Gwen says as she pulls two takeout containers from the bag Darnell brought over. She watches him from the kitchen as he swivels back and forth behind her computer array, eyes fixed on the central screen.

"I mean, why'd they assign you to her?"

"She's the head scientist at a global pharma company doing some sort of cutting-edge research."

"That's cool. What kind?"

"I don't know. Doesn't really matter," Gwen says, opening the first of the tin containers and breathing in the spicy aroma. "Wow, this smells amazing. What is it?"

"It's a spin on beef massaman I've been playing with. You like it?"

Gwen dips her pinky in the sauce and licks it off with a loud sigh. "Oh my God, yum," she says and gives Darnell an enthusiastic thumbs-up. He does a full circle in her chair and then stares at the screens again.

"You spend all day analyzing this woman's data," he says. "Wouldn't it help if you knew her specialty or what she's working on?"

"I don't like too much background on my subjects." Gwen spoons the beef into a plastic serving bowl. "People's jobs, hobbies, where they went to school, their friends and family—all those types of things can distract you from seeing who a person really is. The data that comes through that system is only the good stuff. It tells me everything I need to know."

"I guess that makes sense," he says, leaning forward and reaching out for the keyboard.

"Don't touch that," she warns, then goes back to scraping the inside of the container. When she's got every single drop, she licks the spoon. "Oh, honey, this is amazing. You gotta put this on your menu immediately." She drops the spoon in the sink and pops open the other tin.

"How long has it been?"

Gwen rips off a piece of naan and soaks it in the curry sauce. "I was tethered to her about three months ago," she says before shoving the morsel in her mouth and savoring the pillowy richness.

"Damn, then you probably know all kinds of things about her by now," he says. "I mean, you knew I was a chef ten minutes into our first date."

"That was easy. No normal person knows the difference between daikon and radish."

Gwen brings a platter with the curry beef, bread, chipped plates, napkins, and mismatched utensils into the living room. She sets it on the coffee table, which doubles as the dining area in her small apartment, made all the smaller by the massive computer array positioned across from the couch in the spot where another occupant would probably put a television.

Darnell spins around in the desk chair to face her, but she's already heading back to the kitchen after stealing a piece of beef.

"Radishes are more peppery," he says.

"See what I mean?"

"Is she interesting?" he asks, spooning their meal onto the plates and setting them on the coffee table.

"No, she's *super* dull. Always sticks to her routine. Eat, exercise, shit, work, eat, nightcap. Like clockwork. It just sucks being saddled with such a boring one, even though she's technically classified as a higher tier than what I'm used to."

Gwen opens the cabinet above her sink and moves aside boxes of Hamburger Helper, a few granola bars, a package of Lipton tea, and some cans of soup to reach the wine bottles in the back.

"Red or white?" she yells over her shoulder.

"Red," Darnell replies, then asks, "She ever do anything exciting?"

Gwen reaches past the eight-dollar blend to the fancy Arizona burgundy her boss gave her last Christmas. "Tonight's about as exciting as it gets," she says. "It's date night with the hubby."

"Oh yeah? How do you know they didn't take the week off?"

"Well, let's see," Gwen says, searching the junk drawer for the corkscrew she hasn't used since she started buying the screw-top bottles from the big box store. "What does it say on the left screen?"

"Umm . . . where? There's a bunch of windows."

"Look for one labeled *base biometrics*." She finds the corkscrew in the very back of the drawer.

"Got it," he calls to her. "There's a lot of information here. What's relevant?"

"All of it," she says with a chuckle. "Just start at the top."

"Okay . . . the lines for blood pressure, heart rate, and respiration all have red, upward-facing arrows next to them."

"What time is it?" Gwen asks, flipping the corkscrew around in her hands, trying to remember how it works.

"It's a little after ten," Darnell says.

"So they're probably back from the restaurant by now."

"How do you know? What if she's on the west coast or something?"

"Nah, her melanin production slows every day in conjunction with our sunset, which tells me she's definitely somewhere on the East Coast. And I can tell she's in a large city too, based on the aerosol mass of certain particles she inhales every day."

"Wow. Why do you do all that forensic legwork when you could just look it up?"

"That would take the fun out of it," Gwen says.

"Okay, Detective. What city does she live in?"

Gwen finally gets a handle on the corkscrew and starts opening the bottle. "My first guess was New York—they have the worst air quality out here—or maybe Atlanta. But she also has pretty high mercury levels in her blood, which told me that she's really into seafood. Fresh seafood, like near the Chesapeake. But none of the cities down there are a match for the aerosols. So combining the air pollutant picture with the seafood . . . I'm leaning toward Boston as her home base."

She pops the cork and looks into the living room, where Darnell's jaw is hanging open.

"Told you it's all relevant," she says.

"I believe you. Okay, so what happens now?"

"Now, they have sex."

"Really?" he says, his smile broadening.

Gwen chuckles. "Just keep reading."

"All right, all right . . ." He rubs his hands together as he peers at the screen. "There are more up arrows now."

"Where?" she asks, taking two wine glasses from the drying rack.

"Next to serotonin and norepinephrine."

"What about the cingulate cortex?"

"Yeah, that just lit up!" he yells, pointing at another screen. "So did cerebellum activity."

"In case you're wondering, that's what happens in women's brains during sex."

"Only during sex?"

"Not *only* during sex. Those brain centers are also activated when experiencing heightened emotions or during big decision-making moments. But like I said, she's a creature of habit. And when you add it all up with other data from previous weeks, it tells me that she and the hubby are doing the nasty."

"Whoa," says Darnell. "Amygdala activity just popped. This is getting serious, huh?"

"Check the readings on the screen to your right."

Darnell swivels to face the screen. When he sees the data displayed there, he lets out a small whoop.

"You're such a dude," Gwen says. "What's it say?"

"Breast volume is up, and she's got something called vasocongestion of the genital tissues. What's cutaneous vasodilation?"

"Her skin is getting flush."

"Wait, there's a green down arrow now."

"Which one?"

"Central neurotransmitter," he says. "What does that mean?"

"It means she came."

"Really?"

"Yep."

"Oh yeah," Darnell says, rocking back and forth in the chair, fast at first so its squeak is rapid, then slowing down, little by little, until the squeak stops.

"After dinner, let's see if we can make that first part last a little longer," she says, tipping out a healthy serving of wine into the two glasses and carrying them into the living room.

"Wait till you see the big red arrow I've got for you, baby," he says, smiling as he gets up to take one of the glasses. They clink them, sit side by side on the couch, and dive into their dinner.

After a few bites, he waves a hand over the food to direct its aroma toward him. He wrinkles his nose and takes a small notebook out of his back pocket.

"What are you doing?" Gwen asks as he scribbles in the book.

"The lime is buried. Probably need to double the kaffir leaves. I don't want to forget."

"Your job is so much cooler than mine," she says, scooping up a big bite. "You're like an artist."

"Making food for rich douchebags from Georgetown and Capitol Hill isn't about art. And unless I catch a busboy banging the hostess in the coat closet, I don't get to see anything nearly as spicy as what we just watched."

"Right there, that's as good as it gets," she says, pointing at the array with her saucy fork. "Outside of date night, the best I get outta her is when she has some extra caffeine and her brain chemistry goes all wiggy."

"Do you ever get any say over the type of person you're assigned to?" Darnell asks.

"Nope, never," Gwen says. "At least not at my level. All the high-profile subjects are monitored by data miners housed at the Watergate. That's where the real action happens."

Darnell tips back some wine, but then suddenly points at the screens. "I don't know about that. There's some serious action happening right here," he says, setting his glass down on the coffee table. He moves over to Gwen's array and looks at several red upward-facing arrows. "Looks like tonight's gonna be a twofer."

Gwen smiles and shoves a too-big piece of naan into her mouth. "That's weird. They never go twice," she mumbles between chews. "What's happening?"

"A few readings are pointing north again."

"Which ones?"

"IgE mast cell activation," he says, "basophil histamine release, and something called PAR-2 receptor activation."

Gwen sits forward and sets her fork down on the table, suddenly on alert.

"Hey, what's urticaria?" Darnell asks.

"Hives," she says, jumping up from the couch.

She pushes past him, sits behind the array, pulls the keyboard toward her, and enters a code. A small tray slides out of the right side of the keyboard, and Gwen places her index finger on it. A needle jabs upward from the tray and extracts a sample, and the tray slides home.

Gwen rips open one of the desk drawers and takes out a bright green scrunchie. "Come on, come on," she says, tying back her nest of auburn hair.

Seconds later, the monitors suddenly brighten and the hum from the main computer tower increases. Her fingers begin to fly over the keyboard.

"Are you broadcasting?" Darnell asks, standing behind her and looking over her shoulder.

Gwen nods but stays focused on the blur of information on the screens.

"What's going on?"

"She's having some sort of hypersensitivity reaction," Gwen says, swiping data from the three screens in front of her and entering a blizzard of commands. "Could be something she ate. But it looks like the same amino acid structures in her GI tract from their dinner a few weeks ago. She had no problems then, so that can't be it. Maybe she got stung by something?"

"Is she gonna be okay?"

"Yeah, her respiration and heart rate are fine. It's just . . . weird. This has never happened—"

Gwen suddenly stops typing. She stares at the main monitor, frozen by the readout in front of her.

"I don't believe it."

"What?" Darnell asks.

"Her reaction is being caused by a seminal plasma hypersensitivity."

"A what?"

"Seminal plasma. It's in a man's ejaculate."

"She's having a reaction to her husband's cum?"

"No, she reacting to someone else's," Gwen says, spinning around to face Darnell. "She's cheating on him."

CHAPTER
TWO

SUKI QUIETLY SOBS as ice-cold water washes over her sweaty, flushed body. She knows her neurochemistry is probably all over the place, but she can't help it. All the strategies she prepared in advance to try and keep her emotions in check fled her the second she rolled off of him and the guilt and shame came flooding in.

She takes a few deep breaths and tries to regain her composure, gently rubbing the softly glowing tattoo on her forearm, hoping the signals from it aren't raising any red flags. She focuses on her breathing, forces herself to calm down, and feels like it might be working . . .

Until her lab assistant knocks on the shower door.

She pokes her head out and sees him standing there, naked, with her phone in his hand.

"Something's happening," he says.

She reaches out and takes the phone, which is buzzing almost continuously with notifications. She stares in disbelief as her feed fills with mentions of her, seemingly from all the major Data Harvester watchdog sites.

"Oh no," she mutters as she begins to read.

This happened to her once before.

A few years ago, when flying home from an international pharmaceutical conference, she touched down at Boston Logan to find there was an intense debate raging online about whether she had been exposed to a new influenza variant circulating in the parts of Europe she'd just left. Her data miner at the time noticed a spike in T and B lymphocyte production and started analyzing the possible causes just after she'd taken off from Budapest. And even though it was quickly determined that the cause was bacterial—from a splinter she'd gotten the night before on a deck bar overlooking the Danube—the online trolls who'd been watching her data miner's broadcast created enough of a stir that the flight was quarantined on the tarmac until Suki could be tested and cleared. It was irritating and embarrassing, but eventually she got over it and moved on with her life.

This time feels different.

She swipes her damp and wrinkled thumb up the screen, her fear rising with every mention of "immune system" or "hypersensitivity reaction." That fear turns to terror at the words "affair" and "scandal" and "daughter." And when she sees the breaking news report from the AP Newswire, her whole world tilts on its axis.

The phone slips from her hand and clatters to the bathroom floor. She reels as she rips a towel from the rack and wraps it around herself, suddenly feeling very exposed. Her lab assistant bends down to pick up the phone, but stops short when Suki screams at him to get out. He retreats into the hotel bedroom, and she slams the bathroom door behind him.

She stands there dripping, not moving, looking down at the buzzing phone. When it rings, she kneels and sees it's her boss. She presses the button to silence the ringer just as a text from her husband comes through.

Is it true?

She stares at the message, unable to move or breathe, her skin erupting in gooseflesh. She begins to tremble. Water from her dripping hair beads on the screen, warping the messages from her husband, which just keep coming.

Where are you?

Call me.

CALL ME NOW!

She closes her eyes and tries to think, but the buzzing from the phone against the tiles keeps bringing her back. She claws at the glowing blue tattoo on her forearm, leaving deep red scratches in her skin. She howls in frustration and pounds the shower door with her fist, which alerts her assistant.

"Suki, are you okay?" he calls through the bathroom door.

She doesn't answer, can't answer as she looks down at the last message from her husband.

Whore.

"Suki, you're scaring me. What's happening?" he says more firmly, slapping the other side of the door.

She quickly gathers her phone, yanks the door open—nearly bringing her assistant with it—and leaves the bathroom. He tries to stop her, but she pushes past him.

"What's going on? Please, talk to me," he says, watching her collect her clothes from around the room.

"Here's what's going to happen," she says, struggling to slide her dress over her still-damp body. "I have to get out of here right now before someone figures out where I am. You need to stay here. I mean here in this room. Don't go out for anything. I'll call when it's safe for you to leave."

"What are you talking about?"

"They *know!*" she says, holding up the buzzing phone for his inspection. "Somehow something triggered in my data, which got my miner's attention, which then got everyone else's attention, including our CEO."

"I thought you said that if we stuck to your normal routine—"

"I was wrong!" she says, pulling on her last shoe and heading for the door.

"When can I see you again?"

Suki grabs the door handle and without looking back says, "This was a mistake. I'm sorry."

The hallway and elevator are empty. Suki stares at her reflection in the elevator doors after they close. Disgusted, she wipes the tears from her face and pulls her wet hair back into a quick ponytail. When the doors open again and no one is waiting for her in the lobby, she thinks she'll be able to make a clean getaway.

She's wrong.

As soon as she exits the hotel, lights from several cameras blind her and reporters push microphones in front of her face.

"Doctor Hammamoto, are you having an affair?" someone asks.

Suki waves the question off and looks for a way to the visitor's lot.

"Do you think it's right for a person in your position to be sleeping around?" a different reporter asks, elbowing aside a competitor so she can stay in her cameraman's shot. "What does this say about your judgment?"

Suki pivots to get away from her, but the reporter blocks her path.

"Aren't you ashamed? Don't you have a daughter?"

Suki turns to reply but is cut short when a different reporter starts reading a news bulletin aloud.

"The board of directors of Aevitas Pharmaceuticals has placed their lead scientist, Doctor Suki Hammamoto, on administrative leave while allegations surrounding her infidelity are investigated by the company's legal and ethics team," the reporter says, then holds out his microphone. "Care to comment, Doctor?"

Everyone moves in closer, crowding her from all sides. Suki stands there, frozen in place, struggling to process the information, panic rising as camera lights blind her. The reporters demand a reaction, but she pushes through them and runs to her car.

The shaky footage of her fleeing the scene is on all the major outlets for a very long time.

CHAPTER
THREE

"Senator Martin, the next question is for you," the moderator says, turning to Rosemary. "You've said that if you're elected president, you will support the United Nations Security Council's resolution to broaden the definition of 'people of global consequence,' thereby expanding the number of individuals required to receive Data Harvester tattoos and have their biometrics continually monitored and made publicly available. But many people are concerned, including members of your own party, that this could quickly become a slippery slope. Where should we draw the line?"

Rosemary pushes her sleeves up to her elbows and places her hands on either side of the podium. She wore the red blazer with the three-quarter cuffed sleeves specifically for this question. The Data Harvester tattoo on her right forearm glows a soft blue even under the bright stage lights.

"This is a very important question, maybe the single most important question of our time. Where do the rights of the individual stop and the public's interests start?

"The world is now more connected and complex than at any point in human history. As we saw during the last global economic crisis, the actions of a small group of greedy, reckless people can affect millions and millions of lives. A financial collapse on Wall Street or on the Nikkei Index can lead to people getting hurt everywhere. That's why I support an expansion of who we require to be monitored. Individuals who have the power to influence the destiny of millions of people need to be held in check for the good of us all."

Rosemary counts the seconds during the applause. When it crosses five, she's confident her answer worked, that all the rewrites and arguments with her staff, the lectures from pundits and strategists, the hours of advice from her party's leadership and swing state stakeholders were worth it.

Because the voters are buying it.

She holds up a hand to silence the crowd, making sure her Harvester tattoo is in full view of the cameras. "Furthermore, let me say—"

"That's fine for politicians and Fortune 500 executives," interrupts Governor Nelson, Rosemary's opponent, breaking the debate rules for the third time since they started. "We all agree *those* types of people are extremely powerful and should be watched. You'll get no arguments from me there. But what about doctors, nurses, and teachers? How about pilots and truckers and municipal workers? The blue-collar folks that keep this country turning. They do important jobs that affect lots and lots of people everywhere too. Should we insist that they all get Harvesters and data miners watching them around the clock?"

He scans the crowd with a toothy smile, encouraging a few shouts of approval. When they die down, he continues.

"Isn't this exactly the type of government interference that's led to revolutions in the past?"

Rosemary and her team prepared for this exact moment in the weeks leading up to the debate. She knows that nailing him on this issue could jump her to the front of the pack heading into the convention. She nods along as he speaks, feigning that she's following his line of thought as he hits the same talking points he's been reciting on the campaign trail for months now. She makes sure to keep eye contact with him as he speaks, projecting for the people both here and at home that she's interested in his argument, one that conveniently panders to the very working-class Republicans who represent the voting majority each November.

He's so obvious, and she loves him for it.

When your enemy is making mistakes, don't interrupt them, she thinks. *Damn straight.*

The moderator cuts in, belatedly, before Rosemary's opponent has a chance to continue any further. "Governor Nelson, once again, as we outlined at the start of the debate, you will have the opportunity to respond once Senator Martin has finished her answer."

"It's okay," Rosemary says. "This is exactly what every *normal* citizen is probably thinking when it comes to this topic. So it's not at all surprising that Governor Nelson is thinking it too."

She pauses so the microphones can pick up his exaggerated huff, then continues.

"This issue is incredibly complex and has been debated at great length by leaders, academics, and experts from all over the world. Let me share with you all what we've been discussing.

"First off, I agree that teachers, truckers, and all of the other hard-working Americans the governor just mentioned—and many more like them—are critical to all of our lives. They're what makes this country and the Republican party so great. None of them, however, are afraid of a revolution. In fact, many have told me that they'd happily sign up to be monitored if it makes us all safer. After all, if you have nothing to hide, why would you mind?"

She turns to look at her opponent, letting him squirm, knowing the cameras are all focused on him. After a few beats, she proceeds.

"But no one on the Security Council is talking about expanding the definition to include these types of professions. Of course we're not. We're focused on making sure we include people in the Data Harvester program whose decisions in this country can lead to families losing their homes in Germany and Italy and Russia, or starving and dying in places like Bangladesh and Botswana. And in exchange, we're protecting *all* Americans from having their lives destroyed by bad actors overseas. That's not government interference, that's just good governing."

She lets the applause wash over her, but jumps in before it dies down, making herself a part of the crowd and their voice, not separate from it.

"That's where I draw the line, Governor," she says over the people chanting her name in the auditorium. "We need to balance the personal liberties of those whose actions have a global impact on society against the very real and necessary need for collective safety, transparency, and open access. It's tricky, for sure. And that's why you need serious people involved in these global decisions. To protect Americans! And that's what I'll do when I'm the next President of the United States."

No need to count the seconds this time, she thinks as the moderator works to regain control of the boisterous crowd. When he finally does, he turns to the governor of Arkansas and asks for his response.

"You paint a scary and somewhat convenient picture, Senator Martin," he says, smiling and posturing for the cameras, his go-to move when he's on his heels. "But let's stop talking in generalities and use an example, shall we?"

Rosemary finds it difficult not to let her eagerness show as she suspects what's coming next. It's the cherry on top, and she can't believe he's about to serve it to her.

"Last night, Aevitas Pharmaceuticals, one of the leading cancer therapy companies in the world, suspended their senior scientist, Doctor Hammamoto, due to allegations of infidelity. Doctor Hammamoto's data miner discovered some unusual immune system activity, it was broadcast to the world as part of the standard Harvester procedures, and within hours Doctor Hammamoto was proclaimed guilty by the media and the public. A lifetime's work and a sterling reputation in the scientific community—destroyed in a heartbeat! Do you think what happened to this woman is justified? What she did may have been wrong, but does the punishment fit the crime?"

Rosemary and her team agreed that morning during debate prep that in the event Suki Hammamoto's situation came up, Rosemary would be measured in her response. It would be important that she show sympathy for a high-placed female executive who'd had a momentary lapse of judgment. Can't alienate the moderate women voters, after all. But as she stares across the podium at her opponent's smug face, she struggles to contain herself.

"I think the company is completely justified in their actions," she says. "In fact, I think it's a wonderful example of the Harvester system working." She waves off the start of a rebuttal from him. "Please, sir, don't interrupt me again. Let me finish."

She pauses to let the silence punctuate the moment, hoping the cameras are using it as a chance to zoom in on Nelson's reddening neckline and cheeks, before continuing her response.

"Doctor Hammamoto oversaw international clinical trials at Aevitas, including trials of children with cancer. The minute her indiscretions were discovered and made public, her ability to focus on that important work was compromised. That is irrefutable. What if she misses something in a patient's records that would have made them ineligible for a certain clinical trial? What if she's distracted and doesn't recognize a potentially deadly side effect from one of the drugs being tested? Should we accept the risk to all the patients around the world in Aevitas's trials—the risks to children who are already dealing with cancer—because of Doctor Hammamoto's marital problems?"

That's it. He's done, she thinks, turning away from Governor Nelson as he squirms behind his podium. She faces the cameras.

"We can all feel bad that a marriage is in trouble and sympathize with Doctor Hammamoto for her regrettable mistake. We all make mistakes. None of us are perfect. But it's unreasonable to expect us to sit back and hope that she can keep her eye on the ball under these circumstances. I think Doctor Hammamoto's data miner should be commended for recognizing the abnormality in her data, and the company should be commended for acting swiftly to safeguard the public. This is exactly the type of situation we hope to prevent—and one of the prime examples I'll use at the next meeting of the United Nations Security Council."

The debate proceeds after the applause dies down, but in reality, it's already over.

Nelson struggles to reclaim his earlier confidence in his closing remarks and is met with lukewarm applause as he finishes. Rosemary had prepared a closing argument that was meant to reinforce all the critical tenets of her campaign—the writing is pithy and filled with the types of easily repeatable soundbites designed to fit on TV news tickers and headlines. But she knows from her days as a prosecutor that sometimes it's better to take your foot off the neck of a beaten and bloodied foe lest you risk looking impolite. So she keeps it short and sweet and sticks to the high road.

In a word, she keeps things *presidential*.

Afterwards, she works the rope line longer than usual, making sure to shake every hand and pose for as many pictures as the press wants. When her victory lap is through, she gives a final, big wave to the crowd then ducks inside the waiting SUV. As the door shuts, she slides back in the cool leather seat, closes her eyes, and lets out a deep and satisfying sigh.

"Well, that went better than we thought it would," she says after a few blissful seconds of silence.

"Maybe a little too well," says the man sitting opposite her.

So much for enjoying the moment, she thinks as she opens her eyes and sits forward. The light filtering through the car windows casts him in shadow, which is where he always dwells anyway, his black suit and charcoal turtleneck a perfect complement to the darkness around them. He reaches into a compartment next to his seat, takes out a heavy glass decanter, opens the top, sniffs the contents, and silently nods his approval.

"Tell me," she says, giving a little wave for him to bring on the information—and whatever's in the decanter.

"The Federal Election Commission just announced that they are officially joining the bipartisan push for new data miners to be assigned to both parties' nominees."

Rosemary thumps back in her seat, the euphoria of her debate victory evaporating. "Why the hell are they getting into this? It has nothing to do with campaign finance."

"They're claiming it does," he says, handing her a rocks glass half-filled with a rich brown liquid.

Rosemary takes a long pull on her drink, hoping the scotch's silky burn will help distract her from her racing thoughts and rising fear. She's been working back channels for weeks, trying to quietly squash the bill before it could reach the Senate floor. Now its passage seems all but a foregone conclusion.

"When's the vote?"

"They're introducing it tomorrow," he says. "And my sources say it'll pass fifty-eight, forty-two."

"What?" she gasps. "I've had our allies out there for weeks now, giving the talking points about the importance of monitoring consistency and the value of biometric familiarity. We couldn't keep this thing closer to at least sow a bit of doubt out there?"

"We knew this was a risk," he says. "But there's no other choice now. I mean, just look at tonight. You destroyed that woman from the pharma company. You're the open-access candidate, Rose, because that's what it'll take to win. There's no going back."

She sits quietly, trying to wrap her head around these new developments and the dangers they pose. She stares at her heavy, leaded glass, lost in the scotch's swirling colors as the SUV drives away from the auditorium. The dull sound of sirens from her escort creates an appropriate soundtrack to the alarm bells going off in her head.

But just as she's about to become overwhelmed by the implications of having a new data miner, she's brought back to the present by the man's gentle touch. He takes the glass from her hand and tips out another splash of the liquor. When he tries handing it back to her, she waves it off, indicating that he should do better on the pour.

"No sense in holding back now," she says, watching him drizzle out some more. She sucks it down in two long swallows and sets the empty glass on the seat next to her. "The convention is in two days. After they declare me the nominee and I get saddled with a new data miner, I won't be able to get away with this sort of *unseemly* alcohol consumption anymore."

"You underestimate me, Senator Martin," her companion says. "We've come too far and worked too hard for too many years for it all to come apart now."

"What are you going to do?"

"I'm going to find out who the committee selects to be your new miner. And then I'll dig into their life. Every part of it. Just like I did with your current miner. I'll find the weak points, apply pressure, and get them on board."

"That was easier when I was just a senator from the Rust Belt," Rosemary says, shrugging off her blazer and pulling the comb out of her hair, letting ash-gray and cool blond curls flow over her shoulders. "They're going to watch whoever this new person is closely. It'll be a lot harder this time."

He leans forward and takes her hand. "That's my job, right? Doing the hard things and applying pressure in the right spots?"

He pulls her onto his lap. She straddles him, knits her fingers through the back of his dark, curly hair, and pulls his mouth toward hers. As she kisses him, her Harvester tattoo glows a soft blue in the dark of the SUV. She reaches between his legs and inside the waistband of his pants.

"Hard things, indeed," she says, watching as he closes his eyes. "You better find this person fast. Scotch isn't the only thing I'll have to stay away from once I get tethered to my new data miner."

CHAPTER
FOUR

GWEN PEELS back the corners of her cards and finds pocket deuces. She looks around the table, studying her opponents as they examine their own cards, then flicks a green chip off the top of her stack, sending it spinning into the center of the table and committing her to the hand.

Missy's next to act. She peeks at her cards, looks up, peeks a second time, reaches for her chips, but then checks her cards again before putting a green chip into the center. Afterwards, she takes a sip of her beer and tugs on her left earlobe.

Gwen's played in her dad's game long enough to recognize Missy's tell and knows she's got squat.

Her eyes move over to Harry, who is on the button. He's got his own personal brass section chirping along to Chicago's "25 or 6 to 4" as he looks at his hole cards. His cheeks puff out and his bluster goes up an octave as he reaches for his chips, which Gwen takes to mean he's got something decent. And when he only calls the bet instead of raising, her suspicions are confirmed.

Next is Mr. Riley in the small blind, who tosses his cards into the center, saying he needs to see a man about a racehorse. As he trots off to the bathroom, the betting swings to Gwen's dad, who just checks his big blind and beams at his daughter.

"I'm so glad you're home, honey."

"Save it, old man," she says.

Harry finishes the song with a flourish, sending droplets of spittle over everything. Then with a cackle, he bangs his fist on the table twice, making the chips, cards, and wicker basket of pretzels jump, and deals out the flop.

Ace, deuce, deuce.

Gwen's made four of a kind.

Her dad immediately checks the bet to her.

She plays it cool and checks as well.

Missy is more than happy to let the checked bet continue around, working her earlobe hard.

Harry gets distracted tickling his imaginary ivories on the edge of the table to the opening chords of "Bennie and the Jets," rattling his chip stack until it topples over. As he restacks, he keeps four greenies in his hand and tosses them into the center, making the bet $100 to go.

Gwen's dad double-checks his hand and then calls Harry's bet.

Gwen can't believe her luck. She's never caught a monster like the one she has right now. She checks her cards, even though the deuces are burned into her brain, hesitates a beat or two for effect, then calls the bet.

Unsurprisingly, Missy insta-folds.

"Whoa, whoa, whoa there, kid," Harry says to Gwen. "You see that your pops and I are both in this hand, right?"

"Give it up, Har," Gwen says, grabbing a handful of stray pretzels and throwing them at him. "Your head games used to work when I was younger. But not anymore."

"Oh, excuse me, Ms. Ivy League big shot," he says, picking a pretzel off his shirt and tossing it into his mouth. "Tell me again what you're studying?"

"Biostatistical modeling," she says.

"So you're supposed to be good with math and probabilities and stuff, right?"

"What're ya getting at, Har?"

"It's just that I think your pops here should ask for some sort of rebate or something. 'Cause if you're calling *this* bet with *that* flop, they ain't teaching you the right math, that's for damn sure."

"All right, all right," she says, glancing over at her dad, whose shit-eating grin is his only contribution to the conversation. "Deal already so I can put you out of your misery."

Harry cackles and thumbs a can-you-believe-this-one gesture to her dad before burning and turning the next card.

King of spades.

Gwen's dad pulls the basket of pretzels toward him and starts munching on a few, seemingly unaware that he's first to act. Gwen knows what he's doing—she's seen this vaudeville act before. She wants to play it cool but loses it when he reaches for his third pretzel.

"It's on you," she says, unsurprised by his forced look of surprise and chuckled apologies. He checks the bet.

Gwen follows suit.

Harry belts out a few "Bennie's" at the top of his lungs, a terrible accompaniment to Elton John's masterpiece, and then checks the bet as well.

He deals out another ace on the river.

Dad checks the bet with a pretzel, then takes a bite.

Gwen stares down at the board: ace, deuce, deuce, king, ace. Her pulse rises as the metallic taste of adrenaline hits the back of her tongue. She drums the table with her fingertips. A drip of sweat slides down her back. Harry pushes his chair back and peeks over the edge of the table at his cards like he's peering out of a foxhole. He pops his head up a little bit, looks at Gwen's dad, then at her, and settles behind his peeled-back cards once more.

Gwen tries to ignore him by looking at her dad, who is taking small nibbles out of a pretzel and staring back at her.

She looks at Harry, then at her dad, and then Harry again. *There's no way I'm losing this one*, she thinks, and pushes in all her chips—

Just as the front door flies inward with a thunderous crack.

Officers in FBI windbreakers stream into the room, putting them all under the gun.

Harry topples backward in his chair, his legs catching the edge of the table, sending the cards and chips flying. He's surrounded before he hits the floor.

Missy screams and scrambles from her chair, directly into the clutches of an officer, who grabs one of Missy's arms and spins her around. He has plastic zip-tie rings around both of her wrists in seconds.

Another officer rounds the corner into the hallway that leads to the bathroom. "Out of there, now!" she screams to Mr. Riley. Seconds later, he stumbles into the living room, still trying to zip his fly as he's shoved into a wall from behind.

Gwen's dad thrusts his hands into the air. "My daughter isn't involved."

"We know," an officer says as she hoists Gwen's father out of his chair. "Ray Elliott, you are under arrest for securities fraud."

"Dad, what's going on?" Gwen says.

"I'm sorry, honey" is all he manages as the officer zip-ties his wrists behind his back and pushes him toward the front door, right behind Harry, Mr. Riley, and Missy.

The last officer in the house is trying to tell Gwen something, but she can't hear him over the low buzzing. She strains to listen but can't make out his words. She knows he's telling her something important, but the buzzing intensifies, fills her head, erases everything else.

As the officer turns to go, the room starts to fade and stretch like toffee. Gwen reaches out, pleading for him to come back—

And nearly falls off her couch.

She rolls back from the edge and hears the buzzer calling from downstairs. She glances over at her array, sees that it's almost eight o'clock in the morning, and forces herself to her feet, head swimming. She nearly trips over a stack of empty pizza boxes as she moves to the front door and keys the intercom.

"Gwen, it's me," Evelyn's voice says through the speaker. "Buzz me up."

Gwen hits the button, unlocks the door, and opens it a crack. She takes a quick look around to see if there's anything that can be done to make her place look presentable, but there's really no hope. She's been monitoring Suki Hammamoto almost constantly since the news of the woman's affair broke, and the place is a wreck, with cardboard and Styrofoam takeout containers and trash everywhere. She manages to at least tuck an empty Jack Daniels bottle behind a throw pillow before her boss walks in.

"Holy shit, Gwen," Evelyn says. "When's the last time you got some fresh air?"

"It's been a long week," Gwen says, turning toward her kitchen. "What are you doing here?"

"I came to pick you up. There's a meeting at nine, so you need to get dressed."

"I can't go anywhere," Gwen says, popping a coffee pod into her machine. "Suki's probably up, and I need to be here."

"Doctor Hammamoto isn't your responsibility anymore. You're being reassigned to a new subject."

The news hits Gwen like a snowball to the face. "What? Who's going to watch Suki?"

"No one," her boss says. "Now that Aevitas Pharmaceuticals fired her, she's no longer classified as a person of global consequence. She won't be monitored anymore."

"Evelyn, that's a really bad idea," Gwen says, abandoning her much-needed coffee and walking back into the living room. "I think she's planning something."

"She's not. Now come on. We really need to get going."

"Let me show you some of her readings over the last week," Gwen says, turning to her array.

"You don't need to do that. In cases like this one, we have psych weigh in on the subject's biometrics and projected mental state. They've seen that Hammamoto's exhibiting all the signs of depression and anxiety, but that isn't surprising given that her marriage is now the hottest topic all over watchdog sites and national talk shows. And no one in the department sees any unusual signals."

"They're looking in on her?" Gwen cries. "She's mine! And I'm telling you that I need to stay on her."

"We can talk about this later. Right now, we need to go," Evelyn says.

Gwen is already at her desk. She hits a sequence of keys, and the blood draw tray extends from the keyboard with a hiss. But before she can put her finger on the tray, Evelyn grabs Gwen's wrist.

"Knock it off, Gwen. It's over."

"You're making a mistake," Gwen says. "Who knows what she can do to that company and all the people who work there? We don't know what kind of access she might still have. Friends on the inside. What if she messes with some of their trial data or destroys some new miracle drug that they've been working on. People could get hurt!"

"She's not some supervillain, Gwen. And she's not your father, either," Evelyn adds.

The comment catches Gwen off-guard. In the five years she's worked for Evelyn, her boss has never brought up her father's part in the global economic collapse or his subsequent imprisonment. Or the impact it's had on Gwen's life and career choices. She's stunned to speechlessness, which Evelyn capitalizes on.

"Suki Hammamoto knew she was being monitored and chose to have an affair anyway," Evelyn says. "She made a bad choice and it cost her her career and who knows what else. That's on her. But you did your job, and now it's time for you to move on."

Gwen lets out a deep sigh as she leans forward in her chair, letting her hair hang forward to cover the embarrassment blossoming on her cheeks. After a twenty-second count, she looks up at her boss.

"I'm sorry. It's just . . . you know."

"I do," Evelyn says, heading into the kitchen. She takes the mug from the coffee machine and brings it to Gwen. "Now go get dressed. You're going to be late."

———

TWO MEN ARE SEATED at the table. One has a Conan O'Brien-esque shock of red hair and red eyeglasses. The other appears to be almost a foot shorter than his partner, his bald head gleaming under the conference room lights. A nondescript black cylinder is sitting in the middle of the table in front of them.

"Please have a seat, Ms. Elliott," the imitation night show host says, opening his notebook and unscrewing the cap from his ink pen.

Gwen remains standing. "Who are you?"

"We'll get to that," he says, consulting his wristwatch before scribbling in his book. "First, we need you to log into the system."

Gwen sits down, curiosity winning out over her desire to defy the unknown man's orders. She's heard that a portable array was being developed, but thought it was still in the design stages. Clearly, the government has moved beyond drawing boards.

The device looks like it might be made from some sort of resin or carbon fiber. Light appears beneath Gwen's fingertips where she touches the surface, and a blood draw tray slides out from the right side. As she touches her index finger to the tray, a needle extracts the requisite 0.5 microliters of capillary blood. When she lifts her finger away, the tray slides back into the device, which begins to emit a steady hum.

"Since this is wireless, I assume you're using a TripleDES or maybe a Twofish, at minimum," Gwen says, examining the device.

"Actually, it's a modified Rivets-Shamir-Adelman encryption algorithm," says the bald man.

The cylinder suddenly brightens, and light erupts from the top. At first Gwen can see through the beams of light to the men sitting opposite her, but the stream of light quickly turns opaque and resolves itself into the familiar Harvester interface. Gwen tests moving her head to the side and finds she can see only the razor-thin beam of the projection; the screen is unviewable from any angle other than straight on.

As she positions herself in front of the glowing screen once again, a laser-projected keyboard streams from the device onto the surface of the table in front of her.

"What now?" she asks.

"Please take a look at the data on the screen," the redhead says. "Tell us what you see."

"Why? Is this some sort of test?"

"Yes, it is. And the clock is ticking, so I suggest you get to it."

Gwen shifts in her seat so she can look past the screen projection to the man sitting with his hands folded atop his notebook, staring back at her through his ridiculous red eyeglasses. After a few seconds, he taps the face of his wristwatch and then refolds his hands. His partner's eyes dart back and forth between Gwen and his colleague. After a few more seconds of the silent standoff, Gwen pushes back from the table and stands up.

"No thanks, I'm not interested," she says, turning to go. Just as she reaches the door to the conference room, the bald man jumps to his feet.

"Ms. Elliott, please," he says. "I apologize for the cloak and dagger. My name is Joe Quincy, and my colleague here is Tom Adams."

"What do you want?" she says, turning to face him.

"Your analyses of your previous subject's biometrics were very impressive. Many data miners would have likely dismissed Ms. Hammamoto's mild hypersensitivity reaction as nothing out of the ordinary. But not you, and that's why we're here."

"You were really quick to answer me about the device's encryption," she says, pointing at the black cylinder. "I'll take your test. But first, tell me if I'm right. You're the one who created the algorithm, aren't you?"

Quincy smiles down at his partner. "Very perceptive, Ms. Elliott. How'd you guess?"

"It was the way you said Rivets-Shamir-Adelman," Gwen says, walking back to the table and retaking her seat. "Your voice went up an octave at the end there. I could tell you were excited and maybe even a little proud."

Quincy sits back down, smiling and nodding his head, seemingly enjoying being found out.

"Thank you, Ms. Elliott," Adams says, picking up where he left off. "Now, would you please tell us what you see on the display."

Gwen looks at the female subject's biometric data stream. "Her electrolytes are significantly out of balance. Heart rate and respiration are also erratic, indicative of some sort of physical or emotional stress."

Gwen reaches forward, puts her fingers on the laser-projected keyboard, and begins typing.

"She's definitely dehydrated," she says, her pace on the keyboard increasing as she accesses new screens of data. "And it looks like the chemoreceptor trigger zone of her brain is active, which tells me that her dehydration is probably caused by vomiting. Her gut and bowel chemistry are all messed up too, which makes sense. Diarrhea and vomiting have probably been going on a few days at this point, I would guess. She also has some weird build-up of fluid under the skin on her extremities and back. Probably blistering."

Gwen's fingers fly over the keyboard as screen after screen of data flashes on the heads-up display. Then suddenly, the display winks out and the laser-projected keyboard vanishes.

"What gives?" she says, once again able to look over the top of the now-dormant cylinder to the two men.

"What's your analysis?" Quincy asks.

"A pretty nasty case of sunburn."

The two men look at each other. Gwen can tell her answer surprises them.

"Could it be anything else?" Adams asks.

"Of course," she says, "but I don't think so. Why, what have other people said?"

Adams consults his watch and writes down the time. "We've heard everything from mucosal side effects of cancer therapy to high-level exposure to a nuclear event," he says, closing his notebook.

"No, if it was that, you'd see single- and double-strand breaks in her DNA," Gwen replies. "There was only minor DNA damage, and all of it contained to her skin. So . . . sunburn."

Quincy nods to Adams, who nods back before turning to Gwen. "Ms. Elliott, we represent a bipartisan committee overseeing security and biometric transparency for the upcoming presidential election. You've been selected to be the data miner assigned to the Republican party's presumptive candidate, Senator Rosemary Martin."

Gwen is stunned, uncertain how to react. After a few seconds, she musters a response. "Why the test?"

"People running for office experience unique pressures on the campaign trail, both physical and mental. We need someone who can assess data quickly and accurately. In addition—"

"Thanks, but that doesn't answer my question," Gwen interrupts. "Why *that* test, in particular?"

"Because we're not just looking for someone skilled at data analysis. We're also looking for someone who knows the difference between major and minor problems," Quincy says. "Given the circumstances of this test—two mysterious men with a heavily encrypted, prototype portable array, imposing time pressure on the test taker—the less likely, dramatic answer could have been an enticing choice. But you didn't let any of that cloud your judgment. You followed the data to the correct solution."

Adams reaches down next to his chair and picks up a silver briefcase. He opens it and removes a syringe.

"This is happening now?" Gwen asks.

"Yep, right now," Quincy says. "Don't worry, we've both been trained by a very skilled phlebotomist."

Adams comes around the table. "I'll take your sample to the convention center," he says, "where a technician will conduct the tethering procedure just after Senator Martin's acceptance speech tonight."

Gwen swivels in her chair to face him. He rolls up Gwen's sleeve and wraps her upper arm in a rubber tourniquet.

"In the meantime," Quincy says as Adams guides the needle into her arm, "I will oversee your transition."

"What do you mean?" Gwen asks, wincing as her blood is drawn. "Transition to where?"

"You're being moved into the Watergate."

CHAPTER
FIVE

RED, white, and blue balloons cascade from the rafters to the delight of the crowd in the George Washington University auditorium. Republican faithful, young and old, dance and sing to "Born Free," which booms over the speakers. Rosemary smiles and waves from the podium. She's just wrapped up her acceptance speech, during which she had to pause eighteen times for applause. She grabs hold of her running mate's hand and raises it over their heads for the cameras. The building vibrates to Kid Rock's howls and the crowd's cheers and chants.

After a few more minutes of pomp and circumstance, Rosemary exits stage left into the warm embraces of her senior staffers, red-state colleagues from the Senate, and GOP heavy hitters. As she exchanges *you-da-man*s all around then poses for a picture with the minority leader, a small group of security officers accompanied by a woman in a white lab coat and a redheaded man wearing bright red eyeglasses and carrying a silver briefcase moves through the crowd toward her. Right on their heels is a group of reporters, their press lanyards bouncing back and forth as they hustle toward the scene, microphones in hand and cameras on shoulders.

"Senator Martin, congratulations," the man says as soon as he reaches her. "My name is Tom Adams and I'm from the presidential election committee overseeing security and biometric transparency. I'm here to supervise the tethering procedure to your new data miner."

"Boy, you guys weren't kidding about this happening right after the official nomination," Rosemary says, shaking the man's hand and smiling for the cameras.

"Yes, ma'am," he says, turning aside so the technician can join them. "We know how busy you are, so we'll make this quick."

An event staffer carries a stool and small wastepaper basket to Rosemary, who waits patiently while everyone gets in position for the show. Rosemary's chief of staff steps forward as Rosemary begins to unbutton her jacket. "I'm sorry, ma'am," she says. "We tried to delay this until tomorrow, but the committee insisted."

"No, that's okay," Rosemary says, waving off the suggestion and handing over her jacket. "Best to get it out of the way and get on with winning this thing."

As Rosemary begins to roll up her right sleeve, exposing her Harvester tattoo, a reporter shoves a microphone toward her. "Senator Martin, is this whole thing just a stunt designed by Republicans to make transparency a key issue during the election?"

"I'll remind you that the committee overseeing this is bipartisan," Rosemary replies. "Both parties agree that openness is fundamental to a free and fair election."

Another reporter cuts in. "Some Democrat House members are already saying that if they keep the White House and maintain their majority, they'll immediately introduce legislation that will eliminate real-time data miner broadcasts. Their bill would create a twenty-four-hour delay to allow for additional expert analyses and to avoid broadcasting embarrassing, private information that isn't relevant to the world, like in the case of Aevitas's head scientist. What do you think of their proposal?"

"First off, I don't agree with your assessment of the situation with Doctor Hammamoto, but I am sympathetic to the impact her indiscretion has had on her family." Rosemary makes sure to speak directly into the cameras. "As for the Democrats, I think it's another example of their willingness to throw the baby out with the bathwater. The most recent economic collapse happened overnight. It only took a few hours to destabilize the world economy and destroy countless lives. If we'd had real-time analyses of the perpetrators of that fraud, we might have been able to do something about it. Save our economy and save lives. As a person of global consequence myself"—Rosemary holds up her arm so her Harvester tattoo is clearly visible—"I think this is a reasonable price to pay."

She turns to Adams and nods. He holds the briefcase in both hands facing the technician, who places her thumb against a sensor on the lid. After a quick scan, the sensor emits a small flash and the latches on the lid disengage.

The technician opens the case and takes out a dark metallic ring six inches in diameter and about the thickness of a hula hoop. She slides the ring over Rosemary's right hand and lets it rest against her wrist. As soon as the ring touches Rosemary's skin it begins to contract, its diameter shrinking until it fits snugly against her wrist like a watch band. The ring then brightens to a soft gray and begins to roll up Rosemary's forearm, over her Harvester tattoo and toward her elbow, growing to match the increasing thickness of her forearm. At her elbow it reverses direction, going back down her forearm and shrinking again as it makes one more pass over her tattoo. When it reaches her wrist, a circular port on the top of the ring irises open.

The technician takes a vial of blood from the briefcase and twists it into the port. The ring beeps three times and begins to extract the ruby liquid. As the blood is drawn into the ring, the ring brightens from a light gray to a soft and then bright white. As soon as the vial is empty, the ring flashes between red and white before settling on a bright red and emitting a final series of beeps.

"Can you explain what's happening for our viewers?" a reporter says to the technician, who unscrews the empty vial from the ring and drops it into her lab coat pocket.

"The sintering ring combines the DNA from the data miner's sample with a type of polyvinyl alcohol paste and soft electronic nanoadditives to create an ink," she says as the port on the ring irises closed once again. "It will now use that ink to print a unique, flexible circuit into the senator's Harvester tattoo. The new circuit ensures that only the data miner with the matching DNA can access the biometric data being transmitted by the Harvester."

"And that's what they call tethering, correct?"

"Precisely," the technician says.

The ring has already begun to move up Rosemary's forearm. It slows its crawl when it reaches the edge of her Harvester tattoo and the printing begins.

"What does it feel like, Senator?" a reporter asks.

Rosemary smiles broadly, projecting a lack of concern. "This is my third time. And every time I would describe it the same way. Weird!"

Her tattoo is a bright silver and there's a hint of burnt toast in the air when the ring stops at her elbow. The device rolls back down her forearm to her wrist, completing its final pass, and as it rolls over her tattoo again, the color shifts from silver to the familiar soft blue of an activated Harvester.

"What about Senator Martin's previous miner?" a reporter asks the technician.

"The tethering process ablates the previous miner's DNA from the circuitry, which erases their access to the senator's biometrics," the technician replies.

The ring emits a long, steady beep, flashes green five times, then returns to the dark metallic color it was when the procedure began. The technician touches opposite sides of the ring at the same time, causing it to expand, and slips the ring over Rosemary's hand. As she puts it back into the silver briefcase, she takes a small tube from inside.

"This will help with any irritation," she says as she squeezes out a translucent jelly and applies it to Rosemary's Harvester.

When the tattoo is covered with a thin layer of the salve, she takes a wad of paper towels from her lab coat, cleans off her fingers, and tosses the towels into the wastepaper basket.

She's just moving aside to let the cameramen get a good shot of the briefcase's interior when Adams stops her.

"Don't forget the vial," he says.

The technician shakes her head at her own forgetfulness and takes an empty vial from her coat pocket. She inserts it into its designated foam slot in the briefcase alongside the sintering ring and the tube of jelly. Adams shows the briefcase contents all around for the cameras and then closes the lid.

"That's all, folks," Rosemary's chief of staff says, handing her boss her jacket. But instead of putting it on, Rosemary stands up and slings it over her right shoulder, putting her softly glowing Harvester tattoo on full display.

"Thank you, everyone," she says, following her team toward the exit.

The reporters trail behind Rosemary and the rest of the GOP leadership, shouting questions, trying to get one last soundbite and some additional B-roll for the evening news. So no one sees the janitor beeline to the stool where Rosemary sat during the procedure, or notice when he puts the entire wastepaper basket into the large plastic trash can on his cart.

CHAPTER
SIX

"HEY, EASY WITH THAT!" Gwen shouts as she runs toward the mover who just tossed her keyboard into a cardboard box.

"Sorry, ma'am. Is there a problem?"

"There will be if you broke it," she says, picking up the keyboard and checking it for damage.

"You know this is tagged for recycling, right?"

"No chance," she says, cradling the keyboard to her chest.

"It's going straight to the center in Alexandria," he says, showing her the directive on his clipboard.

Gwen pushes the man aside and rushes out of the apartment. She heads for the elevator until she sees it's full of boxes and crates of her stuff, then opts for the stairs. She goes down them two at a time, passing more moving men heading up, and when she reaches the foyer she races outside. Quincy is standing next to a moving truck and talking on his phone. She runs right up to him, waving her keyboard in the air.

"You can't scrap my array!" she says. She would have said more if she didn't have to pause to suck in a big breath of air. She makes a mental note to work the treadmill back into her schedule.

"Hold on, please," Quincy says to her, then turns his back on her and continues his phone conversation.

Gwen circles around to face him, holding out her keyboard

and raising her shoulders, demanding an explanation. He gets the hint, tells whoever he's speaking to that he'll call back, and hangs up.

"What gives, Quincy?"

"Ms. Elliott, you have a Series Nine array. That generation is being phased out."

"But I know this one like the back of my hand," Gwen says. "I've spent most of the past five years on this machine. Can't you make an exception?"

"I'm sorry," he says. "It's not only that it's outdated. The bigger constraint is that it simply won't work on the Watergate's network. But I assure you that the new models are fully customizable, and I think you'll be more than satisfied once you get everything configured the way you like it." He holds out his hand for the keyboard.

Gwen hesitates a beat or two. She's about to rattle off the merits of her Series Nine when she sees Darnell's car turn the corner onto her street. With a sigh, she runs her fingers across the keyboard's faded letters one last time.

"You could have told me sooner," she says, handing it to Quincy as she brushes past him to meet Darnell.

He gets out of his car dressed in his chef whites and wearing the bright green Crocs Gwen got him for his birthday last month. He's holding a Tupperware container in both hands, but tilts his head toward the moving truck as she jogs up to him.

"Somebody moving?" he asks.

"Yeah, me," she says, taking the container from him and popping the corner of the lid to peek inside.

"What are you talking about?"

"It just happened this morning," she says, cinching down the lid again. "I got a new assignment that's really high profile. Like, super high. So I'm moving to the Watergate. Can you believe it?"

"Wow, congratulations," he says with a quick hug. "When do you start?"

"Immediately." She looks back at the steady stream of her

belongings being stacked inside the quickly filling truck. "We should be out of here soon, which is good. I gotta get going. It usually takes a few days to get a good read on a new subject's baseline. I'm starting from scratch, so I need to look at everything. And I just found out they're forcing a new array on me, which sucks, so I'll have to waste a bunch of time setting that up too."

Darnell nods along, but she can tell that he's not really listening. He keeps rubbing his jaw and looking over at the truck.

"What's wrong?" she asks.

"Nothing," he says, but his lack of eye contact and step back say otherwise.

"Are you mad? Why are you mad?" she says, not letting him off the hook.

"No, it's just—"

"What?" she says, becoming impatient. "You know this is a big deal, right?"

"Yeah, of course I do," he says. "But it's hard enough for us to get together as it is, between your schedule and mine at the restaurant. And now with this . . ."

"Well I wasn't going to say no! Darnell, I was *hand-picked* for this subject by some big-time people. I can't talk about it, I'm not allowed to, but trust me, it's huge. It's everything I've ever wanted."

"What about us?" he says, finally meeting her gaze. "I thought maybe you wanted that too."

It's Gwen's turn to take a step back. She glances down at the container in her hands. After the first few months of dating, back when she'd make sure to hide all the fast-food wrappers and empty Doritos bags before he came over, she slipped up one day and he found out about her terrible diet. Since then, he's always made sure to bring her food.

"It's gonna take us some time to find holes in our schedules where we can do stuff, but we'll find them," she says. "Plus, the Watergate is actually a lot closer to your restaurant than here. It's only a few miles. That's good, right? I'm sure we can make it work."

"That's the problem, Gwen," he says. "I don't want to *just* make it work. I don't wanna be the thing you squeeze into the holes in your day. That's not a relationship."

Behind them, someone closes the moving truck's door and throws the heavy metal latch, ready for the drive across town to Gwen's new home. She looks back and sees Quincy going over a clipboard with one of the movers.

"I can't believe you're doing this now," she says. "I mean, really? Right now?"

"When would be a better time, Gwen? Tell me."

"I don't know!"

"Right, exactly! And that's the problem. You just don't see it." He snatches the container from her hands, opens his car door, and tosses it across to the passenger side. "You know, life exists outside of those screens, Gwen. And you're gonna miss it."

He climbs into his car and slams the door.

She's still standing there, watching him drive off, when Quincy walks up behind her.

"I didn't mention it before, but if you want any visitors, they'll need to undergo an extensive background check before we can grant them clearance. Should I tell Watergate security that you have someone to be vetted?"

Darnell's car turns the corner and disappears. Gwen shakes her head.

"That won't be necessary."

ONCE SHE'S CONFIRMED everything has been collected and has signed a statement to that effect, Gwen walks through the empty rooms and peers out the windows at the neighborhood stretched out below—the deli across the street with the paper-thin pastrami, the drug store with the annoying neon sign capable of penetrating every crack and crevice in her mini blinds, the orange cones holding Mister Mancusso's parking spot outside their building. She takes it all in one last time, then leaves her old apartment behind.

Outside, Quincy points her to a blue Volkswagen Jetta with New Jersey tags. Dual Uber and Lyft stickers adorn the windshield.

"This your side hustle?" she says, curiosity temporarily overcoming her melancholy.

Quincy walks to the passenger's side and opens the door for her. He waits for her to settle in, closes the door, then walks to the back of the car and pops open the trunk. Gwen looks in the rearview but can't see what Quincy's doing. When he gets into the car he's wearing a Washington Nationals baseball cap. He's also ditched his jacket and rolled up his shirt sleeves.

"Well hell, Quincy," she says. "I was worried about our cover, but I see I'm dealing with a real pro."

"Please make sure that appreciation is reflected in your tip," he says, pulling away from the apartment building.

"Seriously, what gives?" She turns in her seat to confirm the moving truck is following behind them. "I was hoping for one of those cool black Suburbans I see you Washington types zipping around in all the time."

"A little conspicuous, don't you think?"

"Sure," Gwen says. "But does it matter? It's not a secret that high-profile data miners work out of the Watergate complex. If anyone wants to, it wouldn't be difficult to just watch and see who's new in the building. And with a little digging, you could probably reduce the variables enough to connect a newly tethered person of consequence to the new arrival."

"We've accounted for that," Quincy says, turning onto a side street. "We send several hundred people in and out of the complex and up and down the elevators every few hours so that it's exceedingly hard to determine who belongs and who doesn't."

"Confusing the signal with a whole lot of noise."

"Exactly. Plus every few days we randomize the entrances and exits miners are allowed to use."

As he takes an exit for the Rock Creek and Potomac Parkway, he glances up at the rearview. Gwen checks her side-view mirror and is surprised to see that the moving truck doesn't follow them.

"Where are they going?" she asks, losing sight of the truck with all her worldly possessions.

"It's part of the protocol," Quincy says. "Your clothing and essentials will be brought to you later this evening. All of your other stuff will be kept in a secure location until after the election."

"Wait. *You're* going to determine what's essential and what's not?" Gwen feigns indignation but feels like she's doing a poor job of selling it. "What if I can't live without my bath oils or yoga mat?"

"I've studied your file and would bet a month's salary that you don't own either of those things," he says. "But if there's something you need, you can put in a request with security."

They drive in silence for a while. Gwen stares out the car window, but the historic sights of Washington, DC don't register with her. She closes her eyes and tries to quiet her mind, but eventually gives up and turns back to Quincy.

"Who's gonna go over all the rules? Is there some sort of briefing or onboarding?"

"You'll find everything you need once you log onto your new array," he says, pointing to the glovebox. Gwen opens it and finds an orange keycard with the number 2273 written on it. "That's your new apartment number. You need to use the south elevator bank. It's through the lobby and down the main concourse, near the back entrance to the building."

"How about you just drop me by the back entrance then."

"Sorry, we need to capture enough of your gait for security. There's a three-tiered protocol to gain access to the floors where miners live: gait, retina, and DNA. We already have your retina and DNA on file. The floor scanners and cameras will create a gait map that we'll use from now on. Today, the keycard will get you onto the elevators."

"How do you have my retina on file? I've never undergone a retina scan."

"Sure you have," he says as he turns onto Virginia Avenue. "Every time you sit down at your array."

Gwen flushes with embarrassment. "Duh, I guess. Not exactly a ringing endorsement for the person you just hired to keep tabs on the potential leader of the free world. Speaking of which, will I at least get some sort of briefing on what's required of me?"

"You just had it," he says, turning into the complex. He pulls the car into the turnabout and parks beneath the iconic Watergate sign near the entrance.

"I don't understand," Gwen says. "I assume with this subject there'll be specific things I need to do. Daily reports and such."

"Gwen, we picked you because you're one of the best," Quincy says, extending his hand. "Just do your job. That's all we expect."

SUNLIGHT FILLS THE LOBBY, bouncing off the polished steel columns and curved bamboo and glass walls, creating a warm and welcoming atmosphere inside one of the most iconic and notorious buildings in Washington. The Watergate transformed from a hotel into a government-controlled facility right after the economic collapse and subsequent passage of the Harvester legislation. It serves as both spill-over office space for congressional staff and housing for visiting dignitaries, ambassadors, and attachés. But it's also home to all the data miners assigned to tier-one persons of global consequence.

Gwen stands inside the front entrance, trying to get her bearings. People are moving throughout the space with what seems like a great deal of purpose. She recognizes at least six languages from passersby, and several more she can't pinpoint from the snippets she overhears. Clicks and clacks from heels on marble echo off the walls and ceiling like modern jazz, without form or flow.

There's no place like home, she thinks as she clicks the backs of her Skechers and makes her way across the lobby.

She tries desperately to walk normally, feeling overwhelmingly gawky and self-conscious with every movement. She's about to turn around, go back to the front entrance, and start over when she sees a sign for the south elevators. *How bad can it be*, she thinks, until she catches her reflection in the rich, burnished bronze of the main desk. That's when she's certain she'll need to explain to security that she doesn't normally walk like a giraffe and beg them to redo her gait analysis.

Following the signage for the elevators, she eventually turns a corner and sees a set of electronic turnstiles stretched across the walkway. She watches as a young man in jeans and an MIT hoodie approaches without slowing or breaking stride. As he reaches a turnstile, its glass doors swing open, letting him through to the elevator bank, then close immediately behind him. Gwen pauses and waits for him to get on the elevator before proceeding, afraid of embarrassing herself by somehow failing to get through the turnstile.

When the man is gone, Gwen walks to the nearest turnstile. The barrier doesn't automatically open for her, but a small panel in the turnstile slides to one side, revealing a card slot. Gwen takes the orange keycard given to her by Quincy, double-checks to make sure she remembers the number for her new apartment, and inserts it into the slot. A mechanism draws the card inside, and the glass doors swing open. When the panel slides shut again, confirming that she won't be getting the card back, she walks through to the elevators, one of which is open and waiting for her. It closes as soon as she's inside.

To the right of the doors, where the buttons for the building floors would normally be, is an opaque glass panel. When she takes a closer look, a green beam does a quick sweep of her face and then winks out with a soft beep. The panel then displays a glowing red thumbprint, at the center of which is a small hole.

Gwen places her thumb over the glowing red icon and feels a familiar prick in her thumb pad. She pulls her thumb away and the elevator begins to move upward, displaying the climbing floor numbers. It stops at twenty-two, and the doors open. She follows the numbers to room 2273, where she finds another opaque glass panel in place of where the door handle should be. Gwen repeats the procedure from the elevator, and the door to her new apartment swings open.

It's bigger than her previous one. The furniture looks comfortable and the kitchen modern. The lighting is warm, and the walls are a pleasing gray-blue. It smells lemony and clean, but a full examination will have to wait. Because all she can focus on as she crosses the threshold is her new array.

It's positioned directly in front of a large window, and the afternoon sun is streaming in and framing the device in a halo of bright light. At first it appears as though she's looking at a single black panel, like a massive flat-screen television affixed to a heavy metal base, but then she sees that it consists of four zero-edge, vertically oriented screens arranged side by side above a similarly black, reflective, and slightly angled desktop surface. There's no visible CPU, but a translucent cable as thick as her forearm snakes from the base, gathers in a few thick loops, and then arcs up to an access panel in the wall.

A red Herman Miller chair sits off to one side. Gwen takes a seat and wheels herself in front of the array. She stares at her reflection in the black screens, tucks a stray strand of hair behind her ear, wishing she had the green scrunchie from her old desk, takes a few deep breaths to calm her nerves, and then gently lays her hands on the desktop surface.

At her touch, the array springs to life. Blinds begin to lower from above, blocking the sunlight streaming in, but lighting set around the edges of the ceiling steadily grows in intensity as the blinds descend, illuminating the apartment in a softer glow. At the same time, the array's four monitors separate and swing away from one another on arms that extend from the base of the terminal, forming a semicircle around Gwen. A green arrow appears on the desktop surface, directing her to a panel that has opened to reveal a blood draw port.

Gwen touches her index finger to the device and feels the prick.

The thick cable leading to the wall panel begins to glow a bright pink and purple, shot through with thin whites and blues, a cotton candy cluster of fiber optics, and the desktop flashes, first white then green. A keyboard and trackpad display appear on the glassy surface, and the four screens show the familiar Harvester interface.

The first thing Gwen notices is that the icon for Suki Hammamoto is still there—but instead of green, it's now amber. When she hovers over it, she finds that it's no longer accessible, just a dead link on the screen. But right next to it is a new one, glowing green, enticing her to click it.

Rosemary Martin. The Republican candidate for President of the United States.

Gwen cracks her knuckles, a wide smile on her face, and reaches for the icon—

Just as her phone rings.

She doesn't want to answer it. All she wants to do is to click the green icon and start digging. But she worries that it could be Quincy with some forgotten instructions or maybe someone from security ready to yell at her for the shitty gait analysis she just provided. She has no choice.

She turns away from the array, plops down on the couch, admiring its firmness, and fishes the phone from her coat pocket.

It's Darnell.

She stares at his picture as the ringing continues, their earlier argument still eating at her. She knows it's a bad idea to let things fester. That'll just make it worse. They should talk this out right away. She should put his mind at ease, apologize for springing the news on him. She should fix it. It would be so easy. But then she looks over at her new array, waiting for her, and can't bring herself to do it. *Not yet*, she decides.

She sends the call to voicemail and silences the ringer.

Back in the red desk chair, she spins to face the screens. A whole new person, a whole new puzzle is ready for her. With a deep breath, she clicks Rosemary Martin's icon and delights as windows pop open on all the screens, brand-new biometric rabbit holes.

She's nearly vibrating with excitement as she sets her fingers on the glowing keyboard and disappears.

Down, down, down.

CHAPTER
SEVEN

SPENCER LEANS against a crumbling concrete pillar as he watches the broadcast from Rosemary's new data miner, the glow from his phone the only light at the demolition site. He thumbs through real-time brain chemistry analyses, through dopamine, oxytocin, and cortisol measurements, through metabolism cross-comparisons. A cornucopia of raw data is being harvested, sifted, and sorted for the viewers. Comments scroll along the bottom of the screen, a combination of scientific discourse and troll vitriol that epitomizes the world's newest spectator sport. It's been less than a day since the tethering at the auditorium, and Rosemary's new data miner has already covered a tremendous amount of ground.

They sure picked the right person, he thinks. And with each table, chart, and waterfall plot, he feels his timeline accelerate. He needs to uncover the identity of this data miner. Soon.

When he hears the vehicle crunching over the debris-riddled pavement, he quickly lowers the phone to his side to hide its light. The car pulls up to the designated spot, its headlights winking out just before it reaches what's left of the warehouse where Spencer is waiting. He slides his phone into his back pocket and walks toward the man getting out of the car, making sure to avoid the piles of rubble and rebar scattered everywhere.

The man is carrying a small wastebasket.

"Zodiac," Spencer calls out, startling the man, who's heading in the wrong direction.

"Sagittarius," the man says, turning toward Spencer's voice.

Spencer waves him over. "Any trouble?"

"Nah, piece of cake," the man says. He hands over the waste-basket. "You got my stuff?"

Inside the basket are the paper towels the Harvester technician used to clean her hands after Rosemary's tethering procedure. Spencer sorts through them, revealing the glass vial she also left for him. *Nice work, my friend,* he thinks as he takes it out and holds it up to the moonlight.

A few droplets of the mystery data miner's blood. That's all he'll need.

"We good?" the man asks, rubbing his hands together and looking over his shoulders.

"We're good," Spencer says, slipping the vial into his jacket pocket and pulling out a gun.

"Whoa, now. Hold on—"

"A grateful nation thanks you."

The bullet does little to erase the look of surprise on the man's face as it pierces his forehead. He falls backward onto a pile of broken concrete and glass, his dying breath leaving his body. He twitches a few times then is still.

Spencer holsters the gun at his ankle. He stays low, scanning the area and listening for any reaction to the gunshot, but not expecting anyone in this neighborhood to raise an alarm. After a thirty-count, he takes a Ziploc bag from his pocket and sprinkles its contents—several white-and-blue striped capsules—around the corpse. After shaking out the last of the narcotics, he puts the empty bag in the wastebasket with the paper towels, steps around the body, and heads for the man's car.

He opens the driver's side door and takes out a Zippo. He dips the lighter into the wastebasket, flicks the wheels, and ignites the paper towels. As the flames grow, he sets the smoking basket on the carpeted floor near the gas pedal and waits. Only when the fire begins to lick at the cloth seat and steering column does he turn to go, making sure to leave the car door open so the night air will feed the flames.

As he walks past the dead man, the metal of the car pops and bends, the fire already starting to consume it. Its glow casts Spencer's shadow across the ground to his parked motorcycle. The soft hum from the electric engine sounds terribly loud as he pulls away from the building, but only until the explosion from the dead man's car shatters the silence of the night.

A FEW HOURS LATER, Spencer pushes a hotel maintenance cart down a warmly lit hallway, his painter's cap pulled down tight, his eyes fixed on the red-and-gold carpet. When he reaches Rosemary's room, he raps his knuckles on the door and stands back. She answers almost immediately.

"We in business?"

"Yes, everything went as planned. No hiccups," he says, closing and bolting the door behind him. He takes off his cap, pushes the cart aside, and follows her into the room. The bed is covered with briefing books and folders. A steaming cup of tea is on the nightstand within arm's reach of a laptop resting on one of the thick pillows. The scent of chamomile fills the room.

"Good," she says, pointing to the computer and rubbing one of her temples. "Because this new miner isn't letting up. I swear they never sleep. The analyses just keep rolling from one to the next, with no breaks in the broadcast. People are loving it."

"Have they found anything?" Spencer asks.

"Not yet. Most of the buzz so far is about the methodology they're using."

Spencer reads for a few seconds before closing the lid and tossing the computer back onto the bed with a sigh. "I'm going to have to move quickly on this one."

"Agreed. So what's next?"

Before he can answer, there's a knock on the door. He holds up his index finger, goes to the door, and looks through the peephole.

"You're about to find out," he says, opening the door and letting in a young woman with a wild mane of twists and curls that go from deep black to pink at the tips. A Loews Hotels staff lanyard swings from her neck, and she has a backpack over one shoulder. In her hand is a green drink that looks to Spencer like liquified grass clippings.

Spencer turns to Rosemary. "This is Maria," he says. "She's with us."

The woman gives Rosemary a quick nod then walks over to the desk. Without asking, she pushes aside a stack of folders, eyeglasses, and Rosemary's cell phone, which is plugged into the desk lamp. She sets her drink down next to, rather than on top of, the paper coaster, opens her bag, and takes out a laptop and a black bifold case.

"You have it?" she says, without looking up.

Spencer takes the glass vial containing the droplets of blood out of his shirt pocket. As he hands it over to her, she holds it up to the light from the desk lamp.

"This'll work," she says.

She opens the black case, takes out a swab, and inserts one end of the swab into the vial. As it soaks up the blood, she reaches into her bag and pulls out what looks like a novelty USB drive with a pink unicorn head for a cap. She plugs the drive into the side of the laptop and twists off the unicorn head, revealing a flat white square, its edges illuminated in red. She dabs the bloody end of the swab on the white square until it emits a beep, at which point she grabs her drink, sits back in the chair, and sucks on the straw.

"Hell of a nightcap you got there," Spencer says.

"Breakfast, actually," Maria replies, holding the cup toward Spencer and giving it a little shake. "Beats the shit outta Starbucks, trust me."

"I'll pass," he says.

Rosemary looks at the laptop screen over Maria's shoulder. "Can you tell me what's happening?"

"It's searching all the major health systems' clouds for a match," Maria says, pointing her straw at the screen. "If the owner of that sample has been to a hospital or clinic in the last ten years, we'll be able to ID them."

"How long?" Spencer asks.

"The scraping algorithm needs to dig through the various cloud platforms and then erase its tracks on the way out," she says. "But it's one of mine, so it'll be quick."

"What if it doesn't find a match?" Rosemary asks.

"It will," Maria says, setting her empty cup down on the desk and getting up from the chair. "Gotta hit the whiz palace."

As soon as she's disappeared into the bathroom and closed the door behind her, Rosemary turns to Spencer. "Where'd you dig her up?"

"We recruited her out of the doctoral program at Berkeley a few years ago. She's mostly been working behind the scenes on other projects."

"Why her?"

"She's talented and fits the profile."

He takes Rosemary's hand and moves over to the edge of the bed, pulling her down to sit next to him.

"You okay?" he says. "You look tired."

"Just anxious, is all."

"I told you, I'll take care of this. You don't need to worry."

Rosemary leans her head on Spencer's shoulder and runs her fingertips up and down the glowing tattoo on her right forearm.

"What's wrong?" he asks.

"When I was watching the broadcast earlier and saw what this new miner was doing, how relentless they are . . . I don't know, it was almost like I could feel them under my skin and inside my head. You can't understand what it's like, the lack of control. It makes me feel helpless and exposed. I hate it."

"I know," he says, kissing the top of her head and hugging her against his side. "Just a little longer, I promise."

Maria comes out of the bathroom, wiping her hands on her pants. Spencer shoots up and takes a few steps away from the bed, feeling suddenly guilty. Luckily his discomfort only lasts an instant because the computer dings and a dialog box appears on the screen.

"Okay, here we go," Maria says, swinging her hips into the desk chair and scooting herself forward. Spencer and Rosemary stand side by side behind her, looking at the smiling image of Rosemary's new data miner in a Princeton hoodie.

"Who is she?" Rosemary asks, her fingers once again caressing her tattoo.

"Her name is Gwen Elliott. She's twenty-nine, DC native, in good health. Scripts for Lexapro and Ortho-Novum. Had her appendix out four years ago without complications. Mother died of BRCA-positive breast cancer, so she gets screened annually. But so far, she's negative."

"That's nice. But what else?" Rosemary asks sharply, leaning forward to get a closer look at the screen.

Maria glares up at her. "I'm sorry, Senator, is this not good enough for you?"

"No, it's not," Rosemary says, then turns to Spencer. "We need more than this."

"And we'll get it," he says, resting his hand on Rosemary's shoulder. "This is just the first step. Now that we know who she is, the rest is easy."

He moves himself so he's standing between the two women and points at the computer. "You've been watching her work," he says to Maria. "What do you think?"

Maria doesn't respond for a few seconds as she looks between Spencer and Rosemary. But then she turns back to her laptop, clicks on a minimized window, and opens Rosemary's Harvester broadcast. After a quick scan, she points to a dense table of information.

"Her initial scrape through the senator's data was almost surgical. She's already moved past the surface biometrics and is now digging into the genomic strata and neuronal behavior."

She swipes through a few menus and then points again.

"Like a lot of the people watching the broadcast—and I'm not talking about the idiots of course, but the serious biohackers and data science wonks—I didn't understand her methodology at first. It's unusual to categorize data the way she does. How she views the various body systems is completely different than any other miner I've ever encountered. Really next-level analytical prowess. In short, she's good. Very, very good."

"How much time do you think we have?"

"At her current rate?" Maria says, closing the laptop lid. "A couple of days. Tops."

She puts the laptop and black bifold case into her bag, zips it up, grabs her empty cup, leaving behind a watery ring on the desk, and heads to the door without saying another word.

Spencer follows her. "Find out everything," he says. "I'll be in touch."

He closes the door behind her and turns back to Rosemary.

"How are you going to get to her?" she asks.

"There's a plan. And you're not going to like this, but that's all I can tell you."

She takes a step back from him. "Are you serious?"

"We need to keep your access to information at a minimum."

"That's unacceptable."

"I'm sorry."

"It's my life, damn it!" she says. "I demand to know right now."

Spencer's phone rings. He glances at the screen and then immediately answers, holding up a finger to Rosemary, who's clearly incensed by him taking the call.

"Yes sir," he says, turning his back on Rosemary and walking a few steps away. He paces back and forth while listening, his eyes occasionally darting over to her, the color in her face draining as she watches him talk to their boss. Eventually he hands her the phone. She tentatively raises it to her ear.

"Hello" is all she manages before falling silent. He stands in front of her and waits. She doesn't say another word or move at all while she listens. After maybe thirty seconds, she holds out the phone to him.

"Your hacker certainly didn't waste any time before reporting in, did she?" Rosemary says. "Fits the profile indeed."

Spencer puts the phone in his pocket and walks over to the maintenance cart. He puts the painter's cap on then opens the door. He's about to back out of the room with the cart when Rosemary breaks the silence.

"Spencer, I'm sorry. I trust you, it's just—"

"Maria's not my hacker," he says, cutting her off. "And I'm not yours."

He pushes the cart out into the hallway then turns to face her once more.

"In the end, Rose, we're all his. You need to remember that," he says, then lets the door swing closed.

CHAPTER
EIGHT

"HERE, let me help you with that," a man says, reaching out and grabbing hold of Suki's suitcase before it escapes. He hauls it over the edge of the conveyor belt and sets it down next to her daughter's little Paw Patrol roller board. They were at her parents' house in Florida for just a few days, so only have a single bag each.

"That's very kind of you," Suki says, adjusting her sunglasses and trying not to make eye contact.

His smile turns to a look of puzzlement. "Wait, do I know you?" He shifts to get a better look.

"Mommy, let's go," Samantha whines, pushing her suitcase back and forth on the shiny linoleum like a vacuum cleaner.

"I don't think so," Suki says to the man, pulling the handle of her bag up and locking it into position, then grabbing Sammy's free hand. "Thanks again for your help."

As she looks for an opening through the impatient crowd swarming the belt, a woman does a double-take. "Hey," the woman shouts. "You're that lady from the drug company."

A man with a luggage cart moves toward the belt, creating a small window of opportunity for Suki and her daughter to squeeze through. She lurches toward it, yanking her daughter, who's distracted by a passenger assistance vehicle driving an old couple through the baggage claim area.

"Oww, Mommy!" she yells as she drops her bag and grabs at her shoulder. "That hurt!"

"Yeah, that's her," the woman says to the people around them. "She's the one who got fired for sleeping around."

"Please, I'm with my daughter," Suki says, picking up Sammy's bag and giving the handle to the teary-eyed girl, who's staring up at the stranger.

"You should be ashamed of yourself," the woman says, waggling a finger. "What kind of example are you setting for that little girl?"

Suki pulls her daughter closer as they try to make their escape, but the woman's ruckus is making it harder to push through the curious crowd. Suki swings her suitcase around in front of her so that she can lead with it and tries to make a path, but Sammy's suitcase keeps getting caught on other people's luggage as they maneuver.

"Slut!" the woman shouts, drawing gasps and some scattered applause as Suki finally escapes the press of bodies. She pauses long enough to scoop up her daughter and stack her little suitcase atop her own, then heads for the escalators.

"Mommy, who was that?"

"No one, honey," Suki says, hoping her little girl doesn't see the tears sliding down her cheeks behind her glasses. She sets her down once they get to the top of the escalator. "She thought I was someone else, that's all."

They leave the terminal through the first exit they find, wind their way through the crowds waiting for ride shares, and head to the customer pickup area. Suki chooses a spot next to a pillar at the far end of the zone, well away from anyone else, and texts the location to her husband.

"Where's Daddy?" Sammy says, jogging around the pillar, her suitcase bumping along behind her.

"He should be here any minute, sweetie."

But Suki's wrong.

She tries to call her husband, but each time it goes immediately to voicemail. She checks their family share app, but it doesn't register a location for him, which means that his phone must be off. She keeps trying to text and call, but after forty-five minutes she gives up and orders an Uber.

Sammy falls asleep on the ride from the airport to their house in Beacon Hill. Suki's nerves are frayed from the encounter in the baggage claim and her husband's mysterious non-responsiveness. *Maybe he got called into work*, she thinks, but quickly dismisses the idea, knowing he'd have left her a message. Everything between them since the affair rests on a razor's edge, but these days apart seemed to have calmed things down. Or so she thought. Now she isn't so sure. Her mind races through the possibilities as they navigate the thick Boston traffic. By the time the driver rounds the corner to their street, she's nearly frantic.

Suki rouses her daughter, sliding her out of the back seat before she's fully awake. She tries to set her down, but Sammy clings to her neck and lets out small sobs at having been yanked from her nap. The driver comes around, removes their suitcases from the trunk, and sets them on the curb. Suki stacks Sammy's suitcase atop her own and pulls them both up the driveway, carrying her whining girl in her free arm. She keys the security code into the keypad next to the garage door and watches as it begins to rise. When it's high enough, she ducks under it and into the garage.

Her husband's car is gone.

Sammy tries to hold on, but Suki sets her feet on the ground and pries her arms off her shoulders. When Sammy drops down into a sitting position on the concrete and bursts into tears, Suki leaves her there, unlocks the door to the house, and heads inside.

She senses the vacancy before she has any definitive proof of it. The very air in the home is somehow different. Hollow and thin and lifeless.

"Sammy, come inside," she yells as she heads into the kitchen.

The blender.

The drawings from the fridge.

The picture of Samantha on the windowsill.

They're all gone.

Her daughter stumbles into the kitchen, rubbing her eyes and making little kid whines of protest. But Suki rushes past her and into the living room.

The Red Sox World Series ball.

A row of books from the shelf.

She runs up the steps and into their bedroom. The closet door is slightly ajar. She rushes over and lets out a screech of despair when she sees only empty hangers on his side.

"Mommy?" her daughter calls. "What's wrong, Mommy?"

In response, Suki can only cry.

CHAPTER
NINE

GWEN SIPS bitter coffee from a Styrofoam cup as she sits in the waiting room and watches the shaky cell phone video of Suki Hammamoto and her daughter being accosted in the airport. The person holding the phone is following Suki as she tries to navigate a hostile crowd, her young daughter in tow. The chyron at the bottom of the screen reads, *Disgraced Aevitas Executive Faces Public Scorn.*

The television volume is off, so Gwen can't hear the news anchor's commentary as the video plays behind him. But she can guess from his smirk and the shrug of his shoulders that his sympathies for the woman do not run deep.

And if she's being honest, hers don't either. She did this to herself.

A prison guard walks in and calls out Gwen's name. She gives him a wave as she swallows the last of the lukewarm coffee, wincing at the metallic taste in the back of her throat. She shoulders her purse, stands up, takes a final glance at Suki's flight from Boston Logan's baggage claim, then follows the guard into a back room.

She comes to the prison every year on her father's birthday, so she knows the drill. It isn't very extensive since he's in a mini-mum-security facility mostly occupied by other white-collar offenders. Though none are as infamous as Dad. No doubt he's a celebrity here—the man whose criminal financial shenanigans ultimately crashed the entire world economy. When it comes to white-collar crime, he wins every game of *What are you in for?*

She sets her bag on the conveyor belt, kicks off her shoes, puts them and everything in her pockets into a bin, and sends it all through the scanner. At the guard's cue, she walks through the metal detector and collects her things on the other side. Once she's situated again, a different guard leads her out of the building and points to the picnic tables at the center of the exercise area.

Her dad stands up and waves as soon as he sees her, his bright orange jumper aglow in the late-summer sunlight. He looks smaller than last year, and his hair is nearly translucent, all traces of gray having given way to white. He throws his arms around her when she reaches him, his stubble sharp against her cheek. She gives him a quick pat on the back then pulls away from his embrace, moving around the table to take the seat opposite him.

"I'm so glad you came."

"It's your birthday," she says, reaching down and unzipping her bag. She takes out two packs of Marlboro menthols and slides them across the table.

"Thanks, honey," he says, slipping both packs into the front pocket of his jumper.

She takes in the deep lines etched on his face and the dark circles under his eyes. "How are you feeling?" she asks.

"I'm fine. You know, same."

"You look tired."

"Nah, just getting over a bug, that's all." He waves off the notion and changes the subject. "You look good. You doing good?"

"I'm okay," she says, shielding her eyes from a beam of light bouncing off the razor wire atop a nearby fence. She wiggles a bit to the left to escape the glare. "Staying busy."

"Oh yeah? What have you been up to?"

"You know . . . the usual," she says, trying to recall what's changed since the last time they spoke. A year ago. "Been dating this guy for a little bit. He's nice. And I moved into a new place. Just a few days ago, actually."

"That's great. Where are you now?"

"Just across town. At the Watergate, actually."

His nose wrinkles as if he caught a whiff of something off. "So . . . you relocated for work, then?"

"Yeah. I got a promotion."

"Good, good," he says, shifting on his bench and touching the pocket with his two new packs of smokes. His thumb traces the top of one of the boxes, but he doesn't take it out.

"You can smoke in front of me, Dad. Go ahead."

"No, no, I'd rather save 'em," he says, folding his hands in front of him. "Congrats on your promotion, honey. That's great."

But she knows he's lying and she isn't in the mood to let it slide under the rug, especially one as threadbare and crowded underneath as theirs.

"What's the problem?" she says.

"Nothing. It's just, I don't know . . . I was hoping you moved in with a friend or something and not just because of work."

"What does it matter, Dad?"

"You're young, is all. You should be doing things other than spending all your time watching other people's lives through some computer screen."

"I'm sorry you don't approve."

"I didn't mean to upset you, Gwen," he says. "All I meant is there's more to it. That's all."

"To what?"

"To life. There's more to life, honey. I don't want you to miss out, like I am."

"Why does everybody have an opinion on how I spend my time?" Gwen says, reaching across the table and pushing one of the packs of cigarettes up out of his jumper's breast pocket. She unzips the cellophane, removes the top portion, and opens the box top. She tips out a cigarette and puts it between her lips.

"What I do is important," she says, turning to her purse and starting to fish around inside. "I make sure people do what they're supposed to do."

"I know," he says. "You're right."

"I make sure people don't do things, or get away with things, that could hurt lots of innocent people." The image of Suki Hammamoto's scared little girl appears front and center in her mind, adding to the bite in her words. "I keep people safe."

"I understand," he says, reaching into his pants pocket and pulling out a box of matches. He hands it across the table to her and watches as she strikes one and lights her cigarette.

"Do you?" she asks, blowing out a stream of smoke. "I mean, you of all people should know that, right?"

He sits back and nods his head, not meeting her gaze.

Their debates used to be spirited due to his unique ability to sniff out any weaknesses in her argument and force her to rethink her position, whatever it might be. Despite how maddening they could be, their arguments were maybe the one thing they had left in their relationship from before his incarceration. But in recent years, she's seen the fight go out of him, until now even that's gone.

"Anyway," she says, sliding the pack and the box of matches back to him. "I moved."

BACK AT HER APARTMENT, Gwen drops her bag near the door, steps around a stack of moving boxes that remain unpacked, and heads straight for the kitchen. She grabs the bottle of Jack Daniels by the neck, pinches a glass from the drying rack, and heads into the living room, where she drops onto the couch.

The rest of the visit with her dad stayed in the safe zone. They avoided any topics that could have led them back down the path of their fractured relationship. He told her stories about her mother—ones she'd heard before, but she let him tell them again anyway, just so there'd be something to fill the rest of the half hour. When the guard came over and informed her that her time was up, Gwen was relieved—and her dad might have been as well.

She pours a few fingers of whiskey into the glass, sets the bottle on the coffee table, snatches the remote, and flops back into the couch. She takes a sip and lets out a deep sigh as she smooshes herself into the cushions. This couch is so much more comfortable than her old one. And it's in the same room as her new array, which is why she's spent every night since moving into the Watergate crashed out on it.

She clicks the remote and the screen on the wall flares to life. She takes a deep pull on her drink as she watches a couple walking on a beach, the crashing of the waves accompanied by a comforting voice listing a steady stream of side effects for which the beachgoers should be on the lookout. When the commercial ends, the local newscaster comes on the air and recaps the day's top stories, including Suki Hammamoto's husband filing for divorce.

Gwen watches the same video she saw earlier in the prison: Suki fleeing up an escalator with her crying daughter. But this time she pauses the feed on a close-up of the little girl's scrunched-up, teary face. She gets up from the couch, walks over to the television, and traces the little girl's head with her index finger. *So small*, she thinks as she takes a swig of her whiskey. She wipes her thumb on the image of the girl's cheek, but the tears remain.

I know how you feel, sweetie, she says, then tosses back the rest of her whiskey and heads to her array, ready to get back to work.

CHAPTER
TEN

MOST PEOPLE THINK ANSWERING questions is the hard part. But answers are easy. Successful politicians always have pocketsful of answers at the ready. What's difficult is listening to people *ask* the questions. That's what truly separates the pros from the amateurs in high-stakes politics.

People are generally terrible at asking questions. Most of the time, a person will ask something, then proceed to editorialize on what they just asked based on their own opinions, experiences, and deep thoughts, often altering the original question entirely by the time they stop speaking. Rosemary discovered early on in her political career that the trick is to see through the noise spilling out of a person to the actual question lying underneath all the words—or at least a version of the question for which she has a prepared and vetted answer. More than a trick, that's the whole ball game. The rest of the time you just need to figure out a way to appear deeply interested in the blather, stammers, umms, and non sequiturs—and look for the right moment to jump in and cut the questioner off.

Which is exactly what Rosemary is doing as she listens to the Ohio farmer with a bit of strawberry jam on his left cheek, one of the suspenders on his overalls unbuckled to make room for his robust middle.

"Do you know what I mean, ma'am?" he finally says, giving Rosemary an opening.

"Sir, you're asking a very important question," she begins. "I agree it's critical to protect local farmers. They are the lifeblood of communities like this one. Farming is not just a business, it's a way of life passed on from generation to generation. And it's under assault. I believe farming needs to be defended in this country. That's why when I'm elected president, one of my top priorities is going to be blocking big agribusiness companies from driving small farmers out of business and ruining the fabric of our nation."

As the crowd claps, Rosemary's watch vibrates—two quick taps against her wrist. She glances down and sees that it's Spencer.

"I'm sure you're wondering *how* I'm going to do that," she continues, ignoring the signal and turning back to the crowd. "I'll tell you. I'm going to start by ensuring you get fair prices on your products so you can compete in a global market. I'm also going to make sure you have access to special, low-interest loans for farms of a certain size and in certain locations—like right here—so you can thrive, rather than just survive."

The taps from her watch come again.

"Now, these steps aren't gonna cure everything or address all the important issues you just brought up in your excellent question, sir. But it's a start. And I hope it demonstrates my commitment to you and your family."

The farmer nods vigorously and claps as he takes his seat at the counter right next to the pie case. Others in the Whistling Pig Diner join him in his applause. Rosemary uses the moment to signal to her chief of staff that they need to wrap up.

Claudia steps forward. "I'm so sorry to have to cut this a bit short," she says, looking at Rosemary to make sure. When Rosemary nods, she proceeds. "But the senator is needed back in Washington. Thank you for your support. And be sure to tip your waitresses generously."

"Thank you everybody," Rosemary says, glancing down at the congealing syrup and thick pork sausage link gone cold on her plate. She never even got to touch her breakfast. And since she was the guest speaker at last night's dinner event in Columbus and had to watch as the wait staff brought and then cleared her equally untouched prime rib, she's been surviving for over eighteen hours on nothing but peanut butter crackers and the gin and tonic she had on the plane yesterday afternoon.

She follows Claudia through the diner, shaking hands and pausing for quick selfies. With a final "Go Buckeyes," she leaves Ohio's best behind and gets into the black limousine waiting for her at the curb.

"What's going on?" her chief asks. "We can't take those farmers for granted. I thought we had another half hour here?"

"Sorry, I needed to get off the merry-go-round for a bit," Rosemary says. "We're back in a few weeks and can make up the time then."

"You feeling okay?"

"Yeah, I'm fine. Just tired," Rosemary says. "But listen, can you please run back in there and get me a muffin or something? I'm starving."

Claudia gets out of the car and runs back inside. Rosemary takes out her phone and quickly dials Spencer's number. It only rings once before he picks up.

"What's going on?" she says.

"Are you alone?"

"Yes, but not for long."

"It's the miner. She's getting close."

"I thought you said we had time," she says, glancing out the window at the crowd spilling out of the diner.

"I was wrong. She's much faster and more efficient than any other miner we've ever seen. It's just a matter of time until she finds something that'll jeopardize us."

"Then we need to slow her down," she says.

"I agree. Which is why you need to look in your top desk

drawer on the plane. Toward the back is a small bag of gummy bears. I need you to eat them as soon as you get on board. It'll be a few hours before you start to feel ill."

"What are you talking about? What are they going to do to me?"

"Nothing major, I promise. Just enough to distract her and give me the time I need to finalize my plans."

"The plans you still won't tell me about?"

He doesn't respond.

Claudia opens the car door and slides into the seat across from her. She holds up a muffin in each hand, and Rosemary taps the banana walnut.

"Claudia's here now. We're on our way," Rosemary says, then ends the call.

"Everything okay?"

"GOP leadership wants to review the Florida trip," she says, breaking off a piece of the muffin and taking a bite.

"Again? My God, how many times are we gonna go over it?"

"I know, but it's getting close to game time and the leadership is shitting themselves."

"How is it?" Claudia asks, pointing at the muffin. It's left crumbs all over the front of Rosemary's suit.

"Tastes a little weird, actually. But it'll do," she says, knowing the Whistling Pig will take the fall for her illness later. *Too bad*, she thinks as she takes another big bite. *This muffin is delicious.*

CHAPTER
ELEVEN

"ARE YOU SERIOUS RIGHT NOW?"

"I'm so sorry," Gwen says, wincing in anticipation of Darnell's reaction to her canceling their date at the last minute. She twists her earbuds in tighter, as if in preparation for an angry blast of profanity that might pop them out of her ears.

"You know I had to beg Trayvon to cover for me tonight, right? And now I'm on the hook for his next three lunch shifts."

"There's nothing I can do, I swear. My subject just got sick."

"People get sick, Gwen."

"I know, but I need to make sure it's nothing serious," she says, swiping a table off the central screen and then keying in a new search command. She thinks that if she can just explain, maybe he'll come around and forgive her, realize that it's an actual emergency and not some bullshit excuse. So she keeps talking.

"Look, I can't get too specific. But I've been looking for a chance to use the Harvester's new polymerase chain reaction analog. They call it *predictive PCR*. It's super cutting-edge, really pushing the capacity of the algorithm."

"Gwen, stop."

"It's still in beta, but this is a perfect opportunity to take it out for a test drive. In fact, I could be one of the first miners to use it, which is really cool."

"Look, I gotta go."

"No, wait," she says, turning herself away from the screens to focus on their call. It felt so good to talk to him yesterday. She'd forgotten how natural their conversations can be, how easy it all comes with him, which is a rare thing in her experience with men.

"I really want to try and make this work," she says just as a search result bings behind her. She claps her hand over the earbud with the microphone, but too late.

"Yeah, sounds like it," he says, his sarcasm crystal clear due to state-of-the-art noise canceling.

"Can we please reschedule?"

"To when?" Darnell says after a pause. "What if your subject stubs a toe or cracks a tooth that day?"

"That's not fair," she says, spinning back around in her chair to see the dialog box that accompanied the notification. "You know how important this is."

"I do," he says in a way that makes it easy for her to predict his next words with near-perfect accuracy. Even so, they sting when they come. "And that's why I gotta walk away now."

"Darnell, wait."

"There's no way I'll ever be able to compete with your job, Gwen. No one will. You are in complete control when you're behind those screens playing with your data. But out here, in the real world, with us normal people, you're not. And that scares the hell out of you."

"That's not true at all," she says, but isn't quite sure what words come next, what evidence she can offer to the contrary. She searches for them, scrambles, but nothing comes.

"Bye, Gwen," he says after a protracted and deafening silence, then ends the call.

She snatches her phone off the desk and hits redial. The call goes straight to voicemail. When she tries again and gets the same result, she throws her phone onto the couch in frustration. But instead of landing softly like she intends, it ricochets off a throw pillow and right into the corner of her coffee table.

"Damn it!" she screams and punches her thighs.

She rips her earbuds out of her ears, drops them on the desk, then goes over to pick up her phone. As she leans down, she sees that a huge crack has spidered across its surface. Instead of retrieving it, she kicks it across the floor with a shriek of frustration.

Before she even realizes it, she's heading for the door. *I gotta get out of here*, she thinks. But before she can leave, her array chimes, and when she looks back, she sees a new dialog box has opened over the stream of data on her main monitor. She wants to leave it behind, if only to prove Darnell wrong. She even unlocks and opens the door to her apartment. But she can't do it. The lure of new data is too strong to ignore.

Fuck it.

She closes the door and walks back to her array. The predictive PCR dialog box is still on the main screen. She takes her seat and swings around into position.

"Holy shit," she says, squinting at the columns and rows of data, her anger instantly gone, pushed aside by the tantalizing mystery in front of her. "What the hell is this?"

She sets her hand on the desk, but all she gets in return is the arrow telling her that she needs to ID herself again before she can interact with the stream. She sets her finger on the blood draw port, and the array welcomes her back with its soft hum and intensified glow.

She begins to broadcast as she slides her fingers up the dark glass surface, flicking the data off the screen and letting new data fill in from the bottom. Proteins, enzymes, and nucleotides flow past as she searches. It doesn't take long for her to find DNA fragments from the *Listeria* bacteria currently wreaking havoc on Rosemary Martin's gastrointestinal tract.

But then she sees something else.

Something she doesn't expect.

Something . . . she can't identify.

Gwen spent a whole year in graduate school running PCRs for her faculty advisor. It's grunt work, but fundamental to biometric analyses. But in all that time and in all the time since, she's never come across the microRNAs she finds in Rosemary's sample.

"Hello there," she says, repositioning herself on her chair, knees folded under her and ankles crossed. She cracks her knuckles and twists her neck back and forth until she gets a satisfying pop. Then she pulls herself tight against the desk and loses herself in the data's absolute, glowing purity.

CHAPTER
TWELVE

THE MAGNETIC ANCHORS DISENGAGE, and four large drones take flight from the roof of a tractor-trailer trundling along Route 66. They climb high into the air, above the tree-lined embankment alongside the highway, and then zip south, their propellers shredding the late-summer air as they gather speed. They maintain a tight diamond formation, their black matte surfaces nearly invisible in the moonless night sky as they approach their destination.

The Watergate.

A few hundred yards away, the drones break formation and speed off in different directions around the perimeter of the building. The lead drone dives down toward the roundabout, skimming above the roofs of the vehicles parked in the visitor lot across from the building's entrance. It pauses briefly as it gets closer, hovering near the entrance canopy and weaving side to side as its pilot times the approach. When a small group of men and women exit the building, the drone angles forward and accelerates through the open double doors.

The ambient beats of the lobby are instantly drowned out by the high-pitched whir of the drone's propellers. Confused people scatter from the invader, dropping to the ground or diving under tables and behind chairs and couches.

A laser shoots from the bottom of the drone. The wide beam

sweeps the area before quickly narrowing its focus to the mirror-like, polished steel surface of one of the lobby's central pillars. The drone races toward it, pulls up, and aims its whirring blades backward just before it impacts the pillar, maneuvering its magnetized feet onto the steel.

It attaches to the pillar with a sharp clang.

Greenish-brown smoke begins to stream from beneath the propellers, which disperse the vapor throughout the space. People grab at their throats, cough, and gag as they try to get away from the noxious air, creating a logjam of terrified people desperate to get out of the lobby, a crush of bodies pressing forward into the fresh outdoor air.

After a frenzied moment, the drone stops emitting the putrid smoke, and its propellers spool down and go silent. A guard pleads for calm, and for a moment, it works. The pushing and shoving subsides as everyone regains a sense of civility, perhaps convinced that the terror is over and they are once again safe.

But the respite is short. The drone starts emitting a high-pitched tone that grows in intensity, louder and louder, drowning out the emergency alarms until—

The drone explodes.

The pillar it was attached to blows apart, sending shards of metal flying through the lobby, puncturing the elaborate teak architecture and expensive artwork. Huge chunks of ceiling collapse to the floor, and water bursts forth from broken pipes that were running up through the destroyed pillar. The scramble to the exit resumes in force, many of the escapees now injured. One woman screams as she sidesteps the growing pool of blood from the decapitated guard who had only moments ago been directing people to safety.

Using video feeds from the other three drones, which have taken up high positions at the corners of the building, Spencer watches the people spilling out of the Watergate. A small crowd collects in the garden just beyond the roundabout, and through the tight press of bodies, he can see someone giving CPR to a woman lying prone on the grass.

Minutes later, the first police car arrives, followed by a convoy of vehicles from DC Fire and EMS. By the time first responders flow into the building, a steady stream of people have already begun to emerge from other exits at the sides and back of the structure. These are presumably the residents of the Watergate—including the data miners.

Spencer types a command on his keyboard, and the three drones turn on their red-and-blue flashers, mimicking the lights atop a police cruiser. This causes most of the people exiting the building to look up, which is important for the facial recognition software. The screens covering the inside of the cargo van now include bright green squares highlighting those faces. Dozens and dozens of the squares turn from green to red in quick succession; none capture the person he's searching for.

Spencer waits patiently. But eventually the flow of people leaving the building stops, and she still hasn't emerged.

"Where are you?" he says, pulling up the broadcast from Rosemary's Harvester.

Even as he watches, the data stream changes to show an image of a double helix, the base pairs that make up the rungs of the twisted ladder denoted in a rainbow of colors. As the image twirls like fusilli in a pot of boiling water, occasional base pairs flash. A new window opens alongside the image, and the words *single-strand breaks identified* appear in real time, the typist having to backtrack to correct some of the spelling.

Spencer curses. *She's still inside.*

He pounds new commands into his keyboard, sending the drones off in a new pattern around the Watergate. As they crisscross outside the building, they shoot out red beams of light that trace the windows on the upper floors, scanning for heat signatures. Spencer keeps an eye on the screens as he adjusts the shoulder straps on his fireman's suit and shrugs on his heavy coat. When one of the drones detects a human form in a room high up on the south side of the building, he notes the location, picks up his breathing apparatus, air tank, and helmet, and jumps out the back of the van.

Jogging through the parked service and utility vehicles that now fill the parking lot, he heads straight to the south entrance. Before he reaches the building, he pulls out a black transmitter with a single red button. He presses the button and watches as his drones pull up and head back toward the vehicle he just left behind. He knows they've reached the van when an explosion rocks the night air.

As a bright plume of fire rises into the sky, Spencer rushes into the Watergate, axe in hand.

GWEN'S FINGERS are a blur as she types and swipes through pivot tables, histograms, scatter plots, and lines and lines of raw data being generated by the Harvester system. Her array's main screen is dominated by a multicolored, twirling DNA helix that she reaches up and taps every few minutes, setting off new streams of information. She's locked in, focused, fully immersed in the flow. The data flashes on her screens, much of it earning the barest glance before it's dismissed as irrelevant, unimportant, tangential. She knows what's she's looking for, and she can feel that it's close. The signal is there; all she needs to do is fish it out from the noise.

All the while, the building alarm continues to blare.

Why are there single-strand DNA breaks? is all she can think, tapping a new section on the helix, sweat beading on her forehead.

The alarm tone shifts, becoming louder, shriller.

It doesn't make any sense. She has no underlying issues that would result in this sort of aberration.

The alarm pauses and the announcement returns.

"There has been an incident in the lobby. All residents and guests must evacuate the building immediately. This is not a drill. All residents and guests must evacuate . . ."

The words finally catch her attention. But she can't leave. Not yet.

She's too close. It's right there.

She can feel it . . .

And then the power cuts out.

"Sonofabitch!" she yells, slapping her palms down on the now-darkened surface of her array. "Come on, come on!"

It doesn't work. She's in the dark. Again.

She takes a few deep breaths, trying to slow her mind and racing heart, and failing at both. *It's in there! I know it!* she thinks, closing her eyes despite the blackness of the apartment. The after-images of the screens slowly fade from her vision, taking the answers with them. She tries to recall them, squinting at the fading data with her mind's eye, but in seconds, everything is gone.

She sits very still in her chair, processing, her mind on fire, itching like crazy, like mental poison ivy. With a deep sigh, she rises from her lifeless array and uses the edge of the desk to guide herself away from the screens and toward the door, under which the glow of emergency lighting is leaking into her dark apartment. Her new home is still foreign enough that she's forced to take small, tentative steps, her arms out and ready to catch her should she stumble.

It isn't until she reaches the door that she realizes she doesn't have her phone.

She turns around and slowly heads back the way she came. When she bangs her shin on the edge of the coffee table, she drops to the floor and sweeps her arms across the carpet, trying to remember which direction the phone skittered after she kicked it. She swipes them back and forth a few times until she catches her pinky finger on a couch leg.

"Fuck it," she says, sucking on her pinky and standing up.

She moves with a smidge more confidence as she returns to the door. Her shoes are waiting in the entryway, and she slips them on and steps out into the hallway.

All is quiet, but at least there's light. Eerie, blood-red emergency light. She hurries down to the elevator bank, only to find that she can't wake the powerless panel next to the doors. Somehow she'd expected there'd be some sort of emergency power system in place for this type of thing, and finds herself oddly disappointed there isn't. Turning around, she heads back the way she came, toward the stairwell at the other end of the hallway.

She's passed her apartment and is only thirty feet from the stairwell door when it opens and a firefighter emerges, dressed in full gear, including helmet, face shield, and breathing apparatus.

"Why haven't you left?" he shouts.

Gwen holds up her hands as if surrendering. "I'm sorry. I was in the middle of something really important."

"Let's go," he says, waving her forward with his axe.

"Actually, is everything okay down there?" she says, pausing. "I mean, if they're gonna let us back inside soon, can't I just stay?"

Just then the lights flicker. On, then off, then on again.

"See, great," she says as the lights hold steady. "I'm going back to my apartment now."

"No, Ms. Elliott, you must come with me!" he yells, his voice urgent. Pushing open the door that leads to the stairwell, he waits.

Gwen acquiesces and starts forward, the itch in her brain coming back hard and fast. She takes a few more steps toward the fireman before she stops, fear suddenly icing up her spine.

"Wait. How do you know my name?"

"They told me downstairs when they sent me up here to get you," he says after a beat. "Come on. Let's go."

"Who did?"

"I don't know," he says, letting go of the door. "A security guard in the lobby."

"What did they say?"

"Look, we don't have time for this," he says, taking a step toward her. "You need to come with me right now!"

She hesitates only for a moment. "No," she says, turning to go. "I think I'll stay here."

He takes off running toward her.

Gwen scrambles back to her apartment door. She's running so fast that she nearly overshoots it; skids to a halt, and swings her face in front of the glass panel, struggling to keep her eyes forward for the retina scanner rather than look at the man rushing toward her. When the red thumbprint appears on the glass, she touches it and hears the lock disengage. She throws her weight against the door as soon as it clicks open, then slams it shut behind her only a breath before the fireman reaches it.

She keeps her eyes on the door as she backs away from it. It rattles in the frame as the man strikes it from the hallway, again and again.

Gwen turns around, frantic. She searches the floor once more for her phone, but even with the lights back on she can't find it. Light flashes from her array, the computer going through its reboot procedure, and she moves to it, hoping to jump on and call for help as soon as it's up and running. Her finger hovers above the closed blood draw port as she waits for the restart procedures to scroll by on the screens.

"Come on, baby," she says as another thwack comes from the front door. She looks back and sees splinters around the frame near the latch.

She searches for anything she can use to defend herself, but even if she had a weapon, most of her stuff is still in boxes. She considers moving the couch in front of the door but doubts she has time, and it'd probably do little to slow the man down.

Another whack at the door, and she can hear the shower of splinters, along with a sharp crack. The door holds, but it won't for much longer.

She looks at the loops of extra cable lying on the floor next to the access panel in the wall—spare cabling in case the user wanted to adjust the position of their array—and does a quick calculation in her head. Is it enough? She scampers to the window, throws it open, and looks down to a balcony two floors below.

It'll be close.

She drops to the floor next to the access panel and flings it open. The cable is attached with a three-inch, threaded gold connector. She twists it loose with a deep grunt, tearing the skin on the palms of her hands, and frees the cable from the wall. She pulls on it as she moves back to the window, causing her array to slide across the floor behind her. She hauls with every ounce of her strength until the array is right in front of her, then turns to the open window and throws the extra length of cable into the night.

When she looks out the window, she can see her cable barely reaches to the balcony down below. She glances back at the door just as another thunderous whack causes a gap to open up around the edges, the frame giving way.

Her heart pounding, she steps up onto the sill.

Turning so she's facing into the apartment, she pulls the cable taut, making the array slide tight up against the window. She stands tall, straightens her legs, and leans back so that she's hanging horizontally, her feet against the side of the building. Grunting under the pressure, she slowly begins to walk her way backward down the outside of the wall, amazed that the Batman cartoons she and her dad used to watch when she was a kid are serving her now in this moment of need.

At least they do until midway down, when her foot slips and her face smacks against the wall. Stars fill her vision as she starts to slip, her bloody palms slick against the thick fiber-optic cable. She struggles to hold on, but it's no use, she's falling, flailing—

She lands atop a teak lounger and bounces onto the steel floor of the balcony. Pain shoots up from her right elbow, but the cushion on the chair saved her from any serious injuries. When the pain subsides enough for her fear to return, she rushes to the double doors that lead back into the building. Luckily, they aren't locked.

She bursts through into some sort of common area. Tables and couches are scattered throughout a well-lit space, with a kitchenette off to one side. Gwen gives no thought to the baskets of fruit, chips, and snacks as she runs through and out into the hallway, then heads left and makes for the stairs.

She's only gone down one flight when she hears the bang of a door slamming open above her, followed by heavy, pounding footfalls in pursuit. She scrambles down faster, taking the stairs two and three at a time. Adrenaline crashes through her, her blood pounding in her ears, and she sucks down air in huge gasps. Her thighs burn from the exertion, and she feels a twinge in her left knee.

"Stop or I'll kill him!" the man screams from above.

Gwen freezes at the sixth-floor landing.

"Petersburg. Cell 132, right?"

She struggles to process what's happening, her head swimming, ears ringing.

"My people on the inside are very good. It'll look like he hung himself."

Gwen looks over the railing. She can see the ground floor below, tantalizingly close.

"We can still make this work," he says. "It's not too late. But you need to listen to me."

"I don't know who you are, but I'm going to the police!" she yells up at him. "I'm sure they're everywhere down here!"

She steps off the landing onto the next step, trying to move as quietly as possible.

"Do that, and your father dies."

Gwen hesitates for several seconds, his last words still echoing around the open stairwell, then takes off running. She practically flies down the last six flights of stairs, her feet barely keeping up with her headlong descent. Above her, she hears her pursuer once again pounding down the stairs after her.

When she reaches the ground floor, she turns toward the lobby, but stops when she sees the other firefighters. They're all over the place. She wants to race over to one of them and beg for help, plead with them to protect her from the man just a few floors above her. But she has no way of knowing if they're here for her too.

She has to get away.

She runs back toward the stairs and out an emergency exit door into the thick, humid night air. The sound of sirens reverberates all around the open field in front of her. A stand of trees is off in the distance, beyond which is the highway. No one is around.

She takes off across the damp grass, driven by the kind of fear that prey must feel with a pursuer at their back. She sprints into the trees before she allows herself to look back even once.

He's not there.

She backs deeper into the darkness of the trees, never taking her eyes off the exit door, expecting the man to burst through it and come after her at any second.

But he doesn't.

She's free.

She drops to her knees and lets herself rest for a few moments. Tears stream down her cheeks and mingle with the cold sweat breaking out all over her body. She brushes them away, sits back against a tree, pulls her knees up to her chest, and starts her analysis.

He knows who I am.

There's something he wants me to do. Something he said we could still "make work."

So—he knows I'm a data miner. Maybe he even knows who I'm assigned to.

Does he want me to expose something? If so, he could have just tried to get me a message. That would have been simple.

He didn't do that.

Instead, he attacked the building. Came for me in disguise. Threatened my dad.

The implication hits her immediately.

This isn't about exposing something. It's about keeping something hidden.

Something major.

Something he'll kill for.

SHIT.

CHAPTER
FOURTEEN

SPRINKLERS RAIN down a steady stream of water on the destruction but do little to wash away the smoky haze that hangs in the air. The fire alarms blare, and orange emergency lights paint first responders and firefighters in a haunting glow as they move equipment in and the injured out of what's left of the Watergate lobby.

Spencer wipes mist from his visor and tries to catch his breath. *She was only a few flights ahead of me,* he thinks, his mind racing. *How did she get away?*

And now she could ruin everything. Years of meticulous planning. All that work, all that sacrifice. All wasted because he fucked up. If he hadn't said her name and tipped her off, this wouldn't be happening. Rosemary would be safe.

He scans the area, hoping to see Ms. Elliott pleading with someone for help, pointing back toward where he's now standing, but she's not there. She's nowhere.

He bites down hard on the mouthpiece of his respirator and heads back to the stairwell. Maybe she exited onto one of the other floors. He's about to bound up the steps when he sees the slightly ajar exit door.

"Tricky bitch," he mutters under his breath as he kicks the door open.

Across the field, he catches a glimpse of someone running toward a small grove, the lights of the highway just beyond it. He's about to give chase when someone calls out to him from behind.

"What are you doing in here?"

Spencer turns to see a fireman holding the door to the lobby in one hand and his respirator in the other.

"I was told to check the exits," Spencer says, glancing outside at the tree line, knowing his prey is escaping.

"No, man, that's not right," the firefighter says. "We need all hands on deck out here. Let's go."

Spencer lets the exit door swing closed and jogs toward the man, but then stops near the bottom of the stairs. He looks up the stairwell and beckons the man over.

"Hold on," he says. "There's something going on up there. Take a look."

Spencer moves aside as the fireman comes over to the steps.

"What are you talking about," the man says, looking up. "I don't see—"

The back of Spencer's axe smashes into the firefighter's helmet. The man crumples to the floor with a choked gasp, his cracked helmet bouncing off the bottom step and landing at Spencer's feet. He kicks it away and listens as the echo from the blow fades up the stairwell. When it's quiet again and he doesn't hear anyone coming from above, he rushes to the exit door, slams it open, and looks outside.

But it's too late.

She's gone.

Spencer pulls the door shut and goes back to the unconscious firefighter who spoiled his chances of catching her. He considers burying his axe in the man's chest, but then tosses it aside and bends over to pick him up.

Blood is oozing from a deep wound above the man's ear, the skin already purpling around the torn edges. Spencer hoists him up into a carry most appropriate for his disguise, and with a final glance at the exit door through which Elliott escaped him, he steps into the lobby. He moves past smoking piles of rubble and through brackish puddles, going as fast as he can, but he feels the unconscious firefighter beginning to slip off the shoulders of his wet jacket. Just as he's about to lose his grip, a young man in a blood-smeared EMS uniform comes running up to him and helps him haul the unconscious firefighter outside.

"What happened?" his helper screams over the sirens of police cars and emergency vehicles.

"Ceiling came down!" Spencer yells, gently laying the man's torso and blood-splattered head down on the sidewalk underneath the Watergate sign. "People are hurt! Get everyone you can over to the south stairwell! Go, go!"

The young man runs back to the front entrance, gathering a few other first responders with him as he goes. A paramedic runs toward Spencer, kneels next to the bleeding firefighter, and starts probing around his head injury. She tries to get Spencer to stay, but he waves her off, makes like he's heading back inside, and then veers off toward the turnabout where District of Columbia fire engines, ladder trucks, and ambulances are parked in a haphazard zigzag.

As soon as he's out of range of the spray coming from the pumper trucks, he strips off his outer jacket. He finds an EMS utility vehicle with its engine running, opens the door, throws his jacket and equipment across the cab, and hops into the driver's seat. He puts the truck into reverse, cuts the wheel, and then heads away from the Watergate.

Once he's merged onto the highway, he fishes his phone out of his pants pocket and dials Maria's number. She answers after three rings, per their protocol.

"Zodiac."

"Sagittarius," he responds, then switches hands so he can drive with his right hand.

"I'm watching the news right now," she says. "What the fuck happened?"

"There were complications," he says.

"Do you have her?"

"She got away."

Maria pauses for a few seconds, then lets out a loud sigh. "Then we're fucked. You gonna make the call or do I have to?"

"I can fix this," he says.

"How? Elliott is probably sitting in a precinct right now."

"She had that opportunity already and didn't take it," he says. "I let her know I'm a threat to her father. As long as she continues to believe that, there's still a chance to get this right."

Maria doesn't say anything, but he can hear her typing furiously, the rapid clicks coming through clearly on the burner phone's tinny speaker. He knows she's probably checking all the police frequencies, trying to confirm his story. He pulls onto the shoulder and turns on the hazards, not wanting to get too far from the Watergate, and waits for her to finish. After a minute, she comes back on the line.

"I don't hear any chatter tied to Elliott. But that doesn't mean we're in the clear."

"You're gonna have to trust me. Don't call him yet."

She pauses for a long beat.

"Fine," she says. "What do you need?"

"Intel. Known friends. Relatives. Lovers. Any place she might go to lay low."

"Hold on," she says, typing once again. "I'm trying to get her phone records."

"She was on foot, so she'll probably be close."

"Okay, I'm in. No recent calls, which is good. Umm . . . she mostly talks and texts with one number. Pulling it up now . . . it's registered to someone named Darnell Wallace. He was the last call."

"Got a location?"

"He lives across town."

"Check his GPS to see if he's home."

"On it," she says, the keys clicking away in the background.

"He's not at his residence. Hold on . . . got it. Sending the address now."

Spencer looks at the screen and sees that he's only a few blocks away from the location. "I'm on my way."

"Seriously, Spencer," Maria says. "At the first sign that this is spinning out of control, I've gotta tell the boss."

"I know," he says, flipping the phone closed.

A news helicopter streaks across the night sky, heading in the direction of the Watergate. When it passes, he turns on the lights atop the truck and swings off the shoulder into Beltway traffic.

Back on the hunt.

HORNS BLARE as Gwen straddles the waist-high divider separating the northbound and southbound traffic. She swings her leg over and crouches down next to the sooty concrete, nerves frayed, sucking in hot air and exhaust. Gasoline fumes burn the back of her throat. She gags and tries to spit away the taste while staring at a long streak of red paint on the barrier next to her. She touches the deep gouge in the concrete and knows she has to get out of the middle of this highway.

She peers over the top of the divider.

All's clear.

The man who came for her isn't there.

Cars and trucks rip by as she waits for a break in the flow of traffic. Even over the roar of the passing engines and the bursts of air buffeting her, she can hear the distant sirens.

A large, two-trailer semi barrels down the road, riding the lane closest to her. She flattens herself against the concrete, arms spread out on either side, and squeezes her eyes shut as it thunders past. The hot blast of air nearly pulls her into the roadway, but she manages to dig her heels into the rumble strip and nubs of rubber stuck to the narrow shoulder to keep herself against the barrier. A few more cars pass and then there's an opening. She scurries across the highway and up the sloped bank to a tree line on the other side.

Pushing her way through pines and scrub brush decorated with greasy fast-food wrappers, broken Styrofoam, and empty cans and plastic bottles, she works her way to the middle where the trees are denser. From this vantage point she can see over the highway to the lights from the Watergate complex. She leans against the rough bark of a dead maple and watches several helicopters circling the scene. Spotlights chase some unseen action on the ground, darting back and forth through the night sky. She keeps watch on the opposing tree line, waiting for her pursuer to emerge and charge across the highway. But after a few minutes with no sign of him, she relaxes. Relief floods through her body, leaving her feeling spent and weak.

She's safe, at least for now.

She begins to wend her way through the trees, having to circle back a few times when standing water blocks her path. It isn't until she jumps across a small gully that she feels the pain in her right knee, finally noticing the injury now that her adrenaline high has dissipated. She probes it gently, wincing at the tenderness around the kneecap. She figures she must have tweaked it in the fall from her apartment window to the balcony two floors below. *Could have certainly been worse*, she thinks as she keeps moving, sticking to paths that take her across level ground.

Eventually the woods give way to the outer edge of a parking lot. She takes a few steps across the asphalt toward a sprawling warehouse, but when a wave of panic hits her she scrambles back to the trees. It feels too exposed. Her eyes dart back and forth across the space. No one is around, no one to call out to. No one to help her in case he comes. She crouches down and waits for the panic to subside.

Sticking to the trees at the edges of the empty lot, she moves around until she can see the front of the long building. Nearby streetlights illuminate a bus stop and a taxi parked just beyond the Plexiglas enclosure. With a deep breath, she leaves the safety of the trees and hobbles to the car, feeling her knee ballooning inside her jeans. She knocks on the glass and wakes up the driver. He looks up at her, rubs the sleep from his eyes, and hits the button to unlock the doors.

She clambers inside and slams the door shut behind her.

"Where to?" he says, starting the engine.

She desperately wants to go to the police. The problem is, she believes the man with the axe. She's spent years evaluating human behavior and is quick to pick a bluff from the truth. His tone was steady, even, and cold. If she talks to the cops right now, that man *will* kill her father.

She needs to go somewhere where she can think. Where she can map it all out and make sense of what just happened.

Somewhere safe.

Somewhere close.

———

MINUTES LATER, Gwen peers through the window of Darnell's restaurant. The front of the house is dark, but she can see lights on in the kitchen. She pounds on the glass until he comes through to investigate. He looks hesitant at first, but then recognition dawns on his face and he quickens his pace.

"What are you doing here?" he says as he opens the door.

"Can you pay my cab driver, please?" she says, pushing past him and into the restaurant. "I don't have my phone or wallet."

"Gwen, what's the matter?"

"Please, just get rid of him."

As Darnell walks out to pay the cab fare, Gwen moves to the kitchen, not wanting to be anywhere near the windows that look out onto the sidewalk and street. She waits for Darnell near the kitchen door.

"Okay, cab's gone," he says when he returns. "Now tell me what's going on?"

"Lock it," she says, pointing at the front door.

"I did already. Gwen, you're freaking me out. What's happening?"

"There was an attack at the Watergate. A man came after me."

"Holy shit. Are you okay?" He steps closer and pulls her into his arms.

"I didn't know where else to go."

He holds her for a few seconds, then gently pushes her away and looks her over.

"My knee's a little fucked up, but I'm okay," she says.

He starts to pull a chair toward her, but she waves it off.

"No, I don't wanna be out here. Too many windows."

She heads through the swinging door into the kitchen. The spicy, rich aroma from the night's dinner service lingers in the air. A thick brisket sits on the prep surface, trimmings piled near a cleaver stuck in the butcher's block. Marvin Gaye's soothing vocals drift from the wireless speaker resting next to a large mortar and pestle.

Darnell leads her to the pantry adjacent to the kitchen. He directs her to the desk chair and then goes into the walk-in freezer and returns with a large bag of frozen peas. She takes the bag and puts it on her swollen knee, wincing at its touch.

"Start at the beginning," he says. "What happened?"

She tells him the story of the last few hours. When she reveals who she's assigned to monitor, he's shocked. And when she gets to the part where the mystery attacker threatens to kill her father, he starts pacing back and forth like a tiger in a cage.

When she's done, he opens a desk drawer and takes out a remote. He turns on the little TV nestled on a shelf next to boxes of pasta, and together they watch the news coverage. All the reporters on all the channels relay the same repeated shreds of information.

Something exploded inside the Watergate complex.

The building had to be evacuated.

Fire and rescue are on the scene.

Several fatalities have been reported.

When one news report shows shaky aerial footage of a body on a stretcher being wheeled from the building, Darnell clicks the mute button, kneels in front of Gwen, and takes hold of the hand not keeping the melting bag of peas to her swollen knee.

"How the hell did they find out about you?" he says.

"I don't know."

"You need to go to the cops."

"I told you, I can't. He'll kill my dad."

"They can protect your dad."

"How do you know that? We don't know who's behind this. I mean, look at the lengths they went to tonight."

"What's your alternative?"

"I need to get back into the system. If I can find whatever they don't want me to discover—"

"Damn it, Gwen!" he says, shooting up from his crouch. "That's not the answer to every problem. You can't solve this one with math and statistics! The only way to keep you and your dad safe is to tell the police everything. And the sooner the better."

She tosses the bag of peas aside and gets up from the chair, her knee buckling slightly as she puts weight on it. Darnell reaches out to help steady her, but she waves him off.

"I can't lose him, Dar," she says, meeting his gaze. "He's all I've got."

He forces her to meet his gaze. "You've got *me*, Gwen. I'm right here."

She chokes back a sob and takes his hand. He kisses her forehead and then each cheek, moist with fresh tears. She pulls him into a tight embrace.

"I got you," he says. "It's going to be okay." He rubs her back, his chin resting atop her head. "You don't have to do this alone."

"Thank you," she says, pushing away from him and wiping her eyes. "You're right. Let's go."

"Good. My car's out back," he says. "Let me grab that brisket I was working on and put it in the fridge. Then we'll get out of here."

As Darnell steps back into the kitchen, Gwen unmutes the television. There's nothing new. No one seems to know exactly what happened or why. But everyone seems to agree that the explosion must be politically motivated.

You don't know the half of it, she thinks.

She's just clicking the off button when a crash sounds from the kitchen. She freezes in place, fear shooting through her.

Glass shatters and Darnell cries out.

She races into the kitchen as quickly as her damaged knee allows—only to find that the man from the Watergate is here, *here*, and he's holding a cleaver to Darnell's throat. He's still wearing the breather over his face, but it isn't connected to a hose or tank, and his fireman's jacket is gone. Blood is streaming down Darnell's face from a gash under his eye.

"Hello again, Ms. Elliott. Let's pick up where we left off," the man says, yanking Darnell's head back to expose more of his neck.

Darnell lets out a yelp that makes Gwen jump.

"What do you want?" she says.

"It's very simple. I want you to stop."

"Stop what?" she says, watching the blood drip off Darnell's chin and onto his chef's jacket, staining his bright white lapel.

"Stop digging into the senator's data," he says. "She's going to do a lot of good—for all of us. But she won't get a chance to if you keep poking around."

"Why?" Gwen asks. "What am I going to find?"

The man shrugs. "In the end, it's nothing important. But as we've seen time and time again, that won't matter. Harmless or not, just by putting the information out there for people to talk about, to ask questions about, or saddest of all, to form their own stupid, ill-informed opinions about . . . you'll destroy the best chance this country has. You can't put a genie back in the bottle. Not anymore. So it's best to just keep it inside."

"I can't stop," Gwen says. "They'll notice. If I don't do my job, my bosses will notice. They'll just assign someone else to her."

"Oh, you'll still do your job," the man says, adjusting his grip on Darnell, whose eyes flutter closed. "Just not so . . . thoroughly. Stick to routine stuff in your broadcasts and everything will be fine. And once the senator is elected, you can move on with your life. You, your father, and even Mr. Wallace here. Everything will return to normal."

Before Gwen can respond, Darnell goes limp, his head lolling forward. The man struggles to keep him from dropping to the floor, and he's forced to lower the cleaver.

That's when Darnell makes his move.

With the blade no longer near his throat, Darnell lunges out of the man's grasp and grabs the heavy mortar. The pestle and ground spices fly through the air as Darnell swings the mortar in an arc. It connects with the breather on the man's face, twisting both it and the man's head sideways. He stumbles backward and falls, clutching at the crushed device digging into his cheek, the cleaver slipping from his hand and clattering away.

"Run!" Darnell screams as he raises the mortar up over his head. He brings the heavy stone bowl down hard, but the man twists out of the way and the mortar smashes to the floor.

Gwen is already rushing through the pantry toward the back door, ignoring the pain shooting through her knee. Behind her, the clang of kitchenware hitting the ground punctuates the growls and grunts of the two men as they struggle. She pushes through both the back door and the light metal screen door into the alley behind the restaurant, then turns and starts hobbling toward the street, praying that someone will be nearby when she reaches it, someone who can help them. But she only takes a few steps before she realizes that she'll never make it. Her knee is on fire, and the pain is creating waves of nausea. She's too slow. If the man gets past Darnell, he'll catch her easily.

"Please be okay, please be okay," she says as she doubles back and forces herself back into the restaurant, fighting with every fiber against her rising panic.

She looks around the pantry for a place to hide. She'd be

trapped if she went into the freezer or the basement, so she opts for the crates of vegetables stacked near the door to the kitchen. She's about to duck behind them when she has an idea.

She returns to the back door, opens it, and unhooks the spring above the screen door. With the spring disengaged, the door flaps wide open. Only then does she scurry back to the crates and crouch behind them, listening.

Darnell roars.

There's a choking sound.

Gurgling.

A thud, then a loud sigh.

Nothing. Nothing.

Nothing.

Then footsteps.

She holds her breath as she peers through the slats in the crates. Someone turns the corner into the pantry, his pace quickening. She can't see who it is, so she stays hidden, praying it's Darnell. The man goes to the back door and out into the alley. After a few seconds she hears him screaming her name.

It's the man from the Watergate.

It's not Darnell.

It's not Darnell.

A moment later he's back in the pantry. Gwen doesn't budge. Doesn't breathe. He kicks something over, creating a loud crash. A can rolls near her stack of crates, bumping against the floorboards next to her. San Marzano tomatoes. The ones Darnell uses for his wood-fired pizzas. *God, I love his pizzas*, she thinks as she stares at the can.

Darnell. Please be okay.

"It's me," the man says.

Gwen nearly screams, then realizes he's talking on a phone. She tries to remain as still as possible behind the vegetable crates.

"She's still in the wind," he says, then pauses, not saying anything, until yelling, "I know!" Another pause. "I'm coming in."

Then it's quiet again.

She strains to hear what he's doing, where he is, but the sudden whoosh of the air vent next to her drowns everything out. She waits for the air conditioner to run its cycle, still not moving, breathing in the thick scent of root vegetables and the dirt still clinging to them from the local farm. When the air finally shuts off minutes later, she doesn't hear anything. She musters enough courage to look through the slats and doesn't see him.

She crawls forward, peers around the side of the crates. She's alone in the pantry.

That's when she sees the haze clinging to the ceiling.

And smells the smoke.

She gets to her feet and forces herself forward, wincing at the pain in her knee, which is even worse than before after kneeling behind the crates. The heat blasts her as she rounds the corner into the kitchen.

Flames are climbing the back wall and licking the ceiling. Black smoke pours from the stovetop, upon which kitchen towels, menus, and bags of food are piled. The dining room is also ablaze, the starched linens of several tables burning and the curtains she helped Darnell pick out now transformed into sheets of fire.

Her lungs seize as she breathes in the thick smoke, so she drops to a crouch—

And sees Darnell, lying on his back, arms and legs splayed out on the floor.

She scampers across to him, screaming his name. He doesn't respond. She kneels over him, turns his face up to hers, so they're looking at one another, but his eyes are vacant. There's a deep dent in his forehead, black and purple around the edges.

He isn't breathing.

She stands up, ignoring the spike of pain in her knee. The smoke is overwhelming. She tries to take a shallow breath, but her lungs spasm and she coughs it back out. Her eyes fill with tears as she grabs Darnell under his arms and tries to haul him back to the pantry. At the first pull, her knee buckles and she drops to the floor, Darnell's torso landing on top of her legs.

With a howl of frustration, she twists to free herself from underneath his dead weight, grabs his left arm, and tries to pull him behind her as she fights for purchase on the slippery floor, her knee screaming in protest.

He's so heavy.

He's not breathing.

She tries not to think about it. Has to keep moving.

The hood on the stove buckles as part of the ceiling crashes down. A piece of hot drywall sizzles on Gwen's forearm, and she slaps it away. Smoke billows around her, and a halo of flames dances above her head.

She pulls Darnell's arm again, but he barely budges. She screams against the strain, and only manages to move him an inch or so. It's hopeless.

She bends down, puts her head on his chest, and closes her eyes, trying to hear anything, detect any movement.

There's nothing.

He's gone.

He's gone.

She looks into his glassy eyes one last time. "I'm so sorry," she sobs, stroking his cheek. She gently closes his eyelids, gives him one last kiss, then hobbles back through the thick smoke to the pantry.

She stutter-steps her way to Darnell's desk, grabs his car keys from the center drawer, and then hobbles to the back door. She's afraid the man is waiting for her, but even if he is, she has to get away from the fire. The heat is already painful against her back. With a deep breath, she peers around the door jamb.

The alley is empty.

She steps out into the night air, but even its coolness against her skin provides no relief. She doesn't turn back. There's nothing to turn back to. Her tears trace fire down her cheeks.

You deserved better.

CHAPTER
SIXTEEN

ROSEMARY PLAYS with a loose button on her pajamas as she reads the draft press release. While her chief of staff's face only occupies a small window in the bottom right corner of the tablet screen, it feels like the woman's anxiety is radiating outward and filling the entire bedroom.

"It's good, but can we tweak the final sentence?" Rosemary says as she paces back and forth in her slippers.

"What do you want it to say?" Claudia asks, chewing on her thumbnail.

"Something along the lines of 'mobilizing all local and federal resources to catch and punish the perpetrators of this heinous act. Bring them to swift justice,' blah, blah, blah," she says, then takes a sip of her tea, wishing it were Macallan. "Add some teeth to it, you know?"

"Sure, sure," Claudia says, only the top of her head now visible in the Zoom window as she transcribes Rosemary's notes. "I'll get Toby to make the edits and we'll put it out there in advance of the morning shows. I'm sure they'll want some time. How about fifteen minutes each for all the major networks?"

Rosemary's reply is swift. "No, I don't want it to seem as if I'm capitalizing on a tragedy to gain some points in the polls. We'll sit this one out for now."

"But ma'am, this is a golden opportunity," Claudia says, leaning into the camera so her face fills the window. "People are going to want to hear from you. And you know the Dems are gonna jump all over this."

"Just put the release out, God damn it," Rosemary snaps. She's been on edge since seeing the first reports about the incident at the Watergate, and she hasn't heard from Spencer since yesterday.

"Yes, ma'am. Understood."

"Claud, I'm sorry," Rosemary says, sitting on the end of her bed and letting out a long sigh. "I'm still getting over that stomach bug and . . . well, you know."

"Don't worry about it. Get some rest."

"Yes, ma'am," Rosemary chuckles. She's about to end the call when Claudia blurts out one last request.

"Oh, but make sure you look at those briefing books I had dropped off. You might get questions about some of the stuff in there during the CNN town hall."

"Okay, will do," Rosemary says. She ends the call and tosses the tablet aside.

Flopping back onto the bed, she closes her eyes. She wants to sleep, would kill for even two hours. But every time she tries, thoughts of the Watergate on fire and the deafening silence from her phone yank her back to consciousness. *Where is he?* she thinks for the millionth time. She squeezes her eyes shut and pinches the bridge of her nose, trying to erase images like the one of a shrouded figure being wheeled away on a gurney in the aftermath of the assault.

It doesn't work.

She rolls off the bed and shuffles to her desk, where a fresh stack of blue spiral-bound books lies waiting for her. Each party's candidate gets expanded security briefings during the run-up to the election, so on top of all her regular campaign obligations, she needs to find a few hours a day to stay on top of the latest intelligence. She sits down, pulls the top book toward her, flips open the cover, and reads the executive summary.

It's a report on North Korea's missile program.

For the first time in hours, she's able to focus on something else. She flips through the intelligence report, which includes images of an undisclosed heavy water refinery hidden deep in the mountains of Kangwon Province. The photographs are strictly exterior shots of the surrounding terrain, indicating that the operative must not have access to the facility itself. As she makes a note to confirm this at next week's intelligence meeting, she hears the back door open downstairs, the squeak from its rusty hinge cutting through the deep silence of the house.

She jumps up from the desk when she hears someone ascending the stairs, hoping it's Spencer. But when the person pauses outside the door and gently knocks, she knows it's not him.

The young man takes a step back and looks down at his feet as she opens the door.

"What is it?" Rosemary says, adjusting her pajama top.

"Apologies, Senator. But you must come with me."

"Right now?"

"Yes, ma'am."

"Where's Spencer? Did he send you?"

"No, ma'am," the young man says, finally meeting her gaze. "The boss said you must come right away."

She steps back into her bedroom and quickly closes the door, trying to hide her surprise. *What the hell is going on?*

She listens to see what the young man does. When she doesn't hear him on the steps heading back downstairs, she knows he's waiting right outside the door for her. Dutifully, just as he was told.

She closes the briefing book. The clock on the desk says it's just after one in the morning. She swallows the last of her tea, then walks to the closet to get dressed. *Might as well get ready for the new day*, she thinks as she reaches past her favorite pair of jeans to her black Louis Vuitton suit.

Something tells her it's going to be a long one.

THEY DRIVE to a storage facility on the northern edge of Washington, DC. The car navigates row upon row of steel units before finally pulling into a multi-car garage located at the heart of the compound. The young man who fetched her watches in the rearview mirror as the garage door descends, waiting for it to be completely closed before turning off the engine.

Rosemary steps out of the quiet car into a hub of activity.

Several men and women dressed in tactical gear are loading heavy canvas bags into the back of a black SUV. Behind them, two people are seated at a folding table working on laptops. Rosemary recognizes one of them as Maria, the woman who first identified Gwen Elliott. Rosemary's driver joins a few others standing next to a workbench. All of them are holding guns.

A door opens and Spencer comes out, wiping at a cut on his cheek with a rag. He sees Rosemary, tosses the rag onto the workbench, and jogs over to her.

"What happened?" she says.

"She got away."

"Shit. What do we do now?"

"The boyfriend's car is missing. We think she has it."

"Wait, what are you talking about?"

"It's a long story. Maria's looking for the car now. We find it, we should find her."

"And the boyfriend?"

"He's dead."

"*What?*" She takes a step away from him, incredulous. The volume in the room drops and people look over, but she's too stunned to care. First the casualties at the Watergate, and now another death on her hands. What was supposed to be a simple mission to bribe her new data miner has turned into an unmitigated disaster.

He grabs her arm and pulls her away from the others.

"Listen to me. It's going to be okay. Maria will find the car, and then me and a small team will go get her. We'll get back on track, I promise."

"Are you insane?" she says, whipping her arm out of his grasp. "We are *way* off the goddamn track here, Spencer!"

His face goes a deep shade of red. He's her closest confidant. They've been in this together since the beginning, so she knows him well. And right now, she knows in no uncertain terms how hard it is for him to hold it together.

She lets out a long sigh and holds her hands up to cue him to stand down too.

"Okay," she says. "But tell me: why am I here?"

"That wasn't up to me," he says, nodding in the direction of the men gathered by the workbench. "Mister Seanwoo is calling the shots now. He wants you here—and he wants Gwen Elliott dead."

CHAPTER
SEVENTEEN

RAINDROPS on the glass form ribbons of water that stream down the windshield, obscuring Gwen's view of the precinct building. She engages the wipers and clears the glass, but can do nothing to clear her mind.

All she can think of is Darnell.

She looks around the interior of his car.

A Starbucks cup with his name written on the side in Sharpie black. A bunch of empty Almond Joy wrappers stuffed in the center console. A stack of his new fall take-out menus on the passenger seat. A rubber-banded bundle of mail, including the latest issue of *Runner's World*.

Her gaze lands on a bright green note stuck to the dash next to the clock. The words *sumac* and *chickpea* are scribbled in his looping script. She rips the stickie off the dash and puts it to her lips. *I'll never taste his food again*, she thinks as she chokes back a sob. *No one will. And it's because of me.*

She turns and buries her face in the leather seat back, inhaling his scent. Tears spill down her cheeks as she squints and shakes her head, trying to erase the image of his dead eyes, the bright red smears and splatters of blood on his chef whites. She hugs the seat as she cries, gently at first and then fiercely, squeezing the sides until her forearms burn and her back starts to ache from her awkward, twisted position. She pounds the headrest and lets out a scream that is short-lived, a dry patch in her throat transforming her howl of agony and grief into sputtering and gasping misery.

She wants to run inside and collapse, grab hold of the first person she can find and not let go until they fix everything. She knows she needs help. This is way beyond her. But she's paralyzed. He killed Darnell, and he said he'd kill her dad too. Who knows—he might have killed her dad already. She has no easy way to find out.

She wishes the killer were here with her now, so she could beg him to stop. She'll give him whatever he wants. He said he wanted *her* to stop. She will. At this moment, she's never wanted anything more in her life.

She twists around so she's facing forward again. She watches as an officer walks out of the precinct. The woman takes a few steps before stopping and glancing up at the rain dripping off the awning. She steps back, pulls her jacket tighter around her, reaches into a side pocket, and takes out a vape pen. The blue tip of the pen glows brightly as she inhales.

Adrenaline crashes through Gwen's body at the sight of the officer. She squeezes the steering wheel until her palms ache, indecision tearing her mind in two. She wants to end it, but she also wants justice.

Finally, after an agonizing minute, her paralysis starts to fade, replaced by what feels like a growing resolve. *This is the right thing to do*, she thinks.

She turns off the engine and steps out of the car, into the rain.

The officer's head is back, her eyes closed, so she doesn't notice Gwen until she's crossed the street and is standing on the sidewalk directly in front of her. Gwen stops at the bottom step and stares up at the cop, who just stares back. After a few seconds of watching Gwen getting rained on, the cop finally breaks the silence.

"Something I can help you with?" she calls from the top of the steps.

Gwen's eyes flash to the woman's holster and the butt of her gun. She wipes rain from her face, happy that the drops are helping to hide her tears. She wants to give up, to tell this person everything, to let the police take over. It would be so easy.

But she can't do it. It doesn't matter if it's the "right thing." Because it's wrong.

She already lost Darnell.

She can't lose her dad.

I have to fix this. No one else.

Just me.

"Hey, are you okay?" the cop asks, taking a couple of steps forward. "Why don't you come inside?"

Gwen turns around and starts back toward the car.

"Ma'am, are you in trouble?" the officer calls out to her.

"I just realized I forgot something," Gwen says as she keeps walking, her pace quickening with each step. "It's not urgent. I'll come by tomorrow."

She gets in the car, shaking so hard that she misses the engine start button a few times. The cop watches her for a few seconds, then goes back inside. Gwen pulls away from the curb with a final, longing look at the precinct doors.

She drives around the neighborhood, trying to figure out how to get back into the system. She can't go back to the Watergate. He could be there, waiting. She needs a plan but keeps coming up empty. After weaving up and down the same streets aimlessly, she turns a corner and jams on the brakes, the answer suddenly right there before her in reflective green.

Arlington, Virginia.

She guns the gas and takes the ramp onto the highway.

GWEN HAS ONLY BEEN HERE ONCE BEFORE. It was last New Year's Eve and Darnell drove home after the party, so she has to circle the neighborhood a few times before she can find the house. She pulls up next to the curb and shuts off the engine. Faux gaslights flicker in the streetlamps, and as she gets out of the car she shuts the door gently, unwilling to disturb the quiet.

She walks up to the house, sees that there are no lights on inside. But when she gets halfway up the driveway, the porch light flares to life, the front door swings open, and Evelyn is there.

"Holy shit, Gwen. The Watergate incident is all over the news," Evelyn says, pulling her into the house and into a hug before Gwen can respond. "Are you okay?"

"No," Gwen says, holding on tight but then reluctantly letting go and turning to shut the door. "I need your help."

"I tried to call you a bunch of times." Evelyn waves her toward the living room. "What happened?"

"It was because of me, Ev. The explosion, all of it. Someone came after me. He knows everything. Me, my dad, the senator." She drops into an armchair and releases a deep sob. "He killed Darnell."

Evelyn is stunned to silence. She stares incredulously, a hand over her gaping mouth as Gwen tells her about the last few hours. She eventually sits down on the couch as Gwen concludes her story, looking worn out just from listening.

"I can't believe this," she says. "How the hell did this guy find you?"

"I don't know. Just that he wants me to stop digging into Senator Martin's data."

"Why?" Evelyn says. "Did you find something?"

"I don't know yet," Gwen says, looking up at the ceiling, trying to remember what she'd been analyzing before the power in the Watergate cut out, thrumming her fist on her forehead. "There was something weird in her DNA, but I need more time to figure it out. I need to get back inside."

Evelyn pushes back into the couch, crossing her legs. She folds her hands on her lap and goes quiet. Evelyn recruited Gwen out of graduate school, and they've worked together ever since, so Gwen knows when to leave her boss alone and let her process. Gwen gets up from the chair and moves to the window, pulling the curtain aside to look at the street. A late-night jogger goes by, but otherwise the world is still.

After a minute or two, Evelyn breaks the silence.

"How do you know I'm not involved?" she asks.

"What?" Gwen lets the curtain fall.

"I know your assignment and all about your dad. What makes you think I didn't have anything to do with this?"

Gwen smiles for the first time since fleeing the Watergate. She moves over to the couch and sits next to her boss. "Oh, I know you do," she says. "I'm here to kill you, in fact."

Evelyn makes a soft "ahh" sound, then takes Gwen's hand.

"First of all," says Gwen, "why the hell would you put me up for the assignment if you were then going to turn around and figure out how to stop me from doing it? You would have simply suggested a lesser miner, like that guy in Florida who only ever gets the Hollywood starlets."

"That's all he ever wants," Evelyn says. "But good point."

"But that's not the real reason. It's because I trust you, Ev. In fact, you're one of the only people I trust right now. And besides, if you did have anything to do with this . . ."

She leaves the last part unsaid, but Evelyn doesn't follow.

"Then what?" her boss asks.

"Then I'd be right fucked, wouldn't I?"

Evelyn gives a wry smile. "I don't know, you already sound pretty fucked to me."

"I can't argue with that. So what should I do? Just . . . just tell me what to do."

"You already know," Evelyn says. She squeezes Gwen's hand and gets up from the couch. "You have to put an end to this."

"I need an array for that."

Evelyn heads for the stairs. "Then let me throw on some clothes and we'll get you to one."

"Where?" Gwen calls after her. "Is there another miner near here?"

Just as her legs are about to disappear up the steps, Evelyn crouches down and looks across the living room at Gwen.

"No, but a Harvester research facility is."

SPENCER SQUEEZES a droplet onto the blue-black metal, then puts the slide on the frame and racks it several times to distribute the oil over the rails and barrel. Soon it glides back and forth with ease. He finishes the assembly procedure, wipes a smear of excess oil off the muzzle, and snaps a full magazine into place.

He's tried yoga, visualization, transcendental meditation, and deep breathing without success. When he was younger, running, boxing, and parkour would do the trick. But American food has taken its toll on his fitness, and as a result, exercising only intensifies his angst these days.

But the gun never fails to calm him.

"I've got something!" a voice calls out, breaking his concentration. He stands up, puts the pistol in his shoulder holster, and jogs over to the table where a man is hacking on a laptop alongside Maria.

"Where is she?" he asks.

"Toll booth south of Arlington," the man says, pointing to the image on his screen.

Spencer looks at the snapshot of Gwen Elliott in the passenger seat of a BMW. "Who is she with?"

"We can't see the driver from this angle," the man says.

"Can we track them?"

"I'm trying to get access to traffic cams in that area right now," Maria says, her fingers working the keyboard, lines of text filling a black dialog box.

Spencer glances at his watch and sees that it's nearly two in the morning. Rosemary is on the phone, pacing, and nodding along to whatever their boss is telling her. He catches her eye, tilts his head to the side, and mouths "what?" Rosemary slowly shakes her head back and forth then turns her back to him, the phone still at her ear.

Not good.

"Are we okay?" he asks her when she finishes the call.

"Not for long," she says. "He's ready to pull the plug."

"It won't come to that," Spencer says, taking her hand and pulling her toward him. She resists at first, but then lets herself get close. He traces the blue tattoo on her forearm, his index finger following the intricate swirls on her pale skin.

"Spencer," she whispers. "Tell me we're going to be okay."

"We will," he says, cupping her chin and forcing her to look him in the eye. "I promise."

"I'm in!" Maria shouts.

Spencer and Rosemary move behind Maria and watch over her shoulders as a grid of black-and-white video feeds fills her laptop screen. Before long, a still frame of the BMW outlined in red takes up the top position on the screen. In it, Gwen Elliott is visible, but the driver's face is partially obscured due to the high position of the camera.

A minute later, a camera captures the car going through a different intersection.

"Another one," Maria says. "Just west of where the first one was taken."

"Who is that?" Spencer says. This camera has captured a much clearer picture of the driver, but it turns out they don't need the facial recognition software.

"Her name is Evelyn Young," Rosemary says, slapping the back of Maria's chair. "I was on a panel with her last year on ethics and data privacy, or something like that. If I remember correctly, she was involved in the original Harvester designs."

"She was also Elliott's boss," Spencer says.

Rosemary shakes her head. "Why would she go to her?"

Spencer turns away from the screens so he can think, absent-mindedly adjusting his newly oiled gun in its holster. He unbuckles the strap, pulls it tight against his shoulder, then buckles it back into the same hole as before. Meanwhile, Maria gets another ping from a traffic camera. They've captured another image of Gwen and Evelyn, this one at a four-way stop.

"Looks like they're heading east toward the industrial parks," she says.

And that's when Spencer figures it out.

"Elliott went to her because she can get her back into the system," he says. "She's taking her to a Harvester array."

"Right!" says Maria, punching in a sequence of keystrokes that minimizes all the traffic camera images and opens a new, blank dialog box.

"Can you find it?" he says.

"Give me a second." Maria types in a string of characters and numbers that probably make sense to only a few, and certainly no one in the room except maybe the other hacker sitting next to her, though the puzzled look on his face indicates otherwise. "I'm searching Dominion Energy's records for properties in Ashton Heights, which is dead ahead of them."

"Why the electric company?" Rosemary asks.

"Arrays draw a significant amount of power," Spencer explains. "If we can pinpoint a location with unusual energy consumption—"

"Got it!" Maria shouts. "A warehouse near their location fits the bill. Huge monthly kilowatts flowing into this bad boy."

"Let's go!" Spencer shouts, sending the rest of the crew into motion. He turns back to Maria. "Keep on them and let me know right away if they change course."

She nods and keeps working.

Before dashing off to the SUV, Spencer pulls Rosemary aside. "Don't worry, I'll take care of it," he says, brushing his thumb across her cheek.

She puts her hand atop his. "You know what he'll do if you don't, right?"

Spencer doesn't respond. He doesn't have to.

They both know.

CHAPTER
NINETEEN

THE SECURITY GATEHOUSE IS UNMANNED, and the parking lot is empty. Heavy wooden barrier arms block entry to the industrial park.

"Thanks again for driving," Gwen says, dropping the now-warm ice pack to the floor and gently probing her knee with her fingers.

"Listen, when we're done here I'll call the prison," Evelyn says, rooting around inside her purse and pulling out a badge and lanyard. "Given my position, I might be able to convince them to put some extra security around your father until this gets sorted out."

"That would be great," Gwen says, flexing her injured leg up and down.

Evelyn lowers her window and touches her badge to the card reader. There's a soft beep as the light on the reader changes from red to green and the wooden arms swing upward. She puts the car in gear and slowly pulls through the gate.

"When's the last time you visited him?" she asks.

"Last week."

"Oh yeah? How'd it go?"

"Same as always. The conversation mostly stayed in the safe

zone, until he found an opening to jump on me about my screwed-up priorities and how I'm missing out on life."

"I'm sure he's just worried about you," Evelyn says, slowing down for the speed bumps.

"Yeah, maybe. It was fine."

"He's not entirely wrong. You can be a *tad* obsessive."

"I take my job seriously. What's wrong with that?"

"Nothing at all. But it's possible to be great at your job *and* still have a life."

"Oh yeah," Gwen says, "and how'd that work out for me and Darnell?"

She regrets her words as soon as she says them. Evelyn's sticking her neck out for her and doesn't deserve cheap sarcasm in return. Darnell doesn't deserve it either, being used as a rhetorical jab mere hours after he was murdered.

"Fuck, I'm sorry," Gwen says. "I shouldn't have said that. I do understand what you're saying. But right now, after everything that's happened . . ."

"It's okay," Evelyn says, reaching over and giving Gwen's hand a gentle squeeze.

After a few seconds of awkward silence, Gwen tries again. "I just think it's ironic, is all, him telling me I'm missing out on life. Because he's the one who's missing out."

"Not by choice."

"No, but also yes. It's his fault he's in prison. His choices. He and his partners brought the whole financial system crashing down!" Gwen shakes her head. "And yet somehow, through my anger and shame, I still found a way to blame myself."

"You can't blame yourself for your father's actions," Evelyn says, parking in a spot near a loading dock. She kills the engine and looks over to Gwen.

"Why not? All the signs were there," Gwen says. "It was clear as day that he and his buddies were up to something. I should have seen it. Maybe I didn't want to. Who knows?"

"You were just a kid," Evelyn says. "No one else saw it either.

Not the IRS, bank regulators, the treasury department . . . No one had any idea what they were up to until it was too late."

"That's the whole point," Gwen insists. "No one saw it, because no one was watching. And the result was a once-in-a-generation, global economic collapse. That's all the proof anyone should need that we *must* keep an eye on people like my dad to make sure nothing like that ever happens again. My eyes were shut back then. Now I keep them wide open. That's why I take my job so seriously. I'm trying to make up for what I did. And in a way, for what he did."

She reaches for the door handle to get out of the car, but Evelyn grabs her arm.

"You realize that even if the Harvesters existed back then, and someone was watching your dad, that doesn't mean they would have known what he was doing. The system lets us see a lot of things, but it doesn't show us everything."

Gwen shakes her head. "I think you're wrong. I think it does show us everything—if you know what to look for."

———

THEY WALK UP the loading dock ramp. Next to the large steel garage door is a regular door, but there's no signage to indicate what's behind either of them. A device is mounted to the brick wall near the handle like the one outside Gwen's Watergate apartment.

Evelyn leans over so that she's looking into the reflective surface. A beam of light scans her face, then with a soft beep a red thumbprint appears on its surface. She places her thumb on the glowing print and the door lock disengages.

As they enter the warehouse, the ceiling lights flicker to life. The center of the space is the exact picture Gwen has in her mind when she thinks of a warehouse—high shelves filled with boxes, crates, and containers—but the walls are lined with workbenches piled high with what look like disassembled Harvester arrays, spools of fiber-optic wiring, and nests of circuitry, wires, and computer boards. Evelyn leads Gwen around the perimeter, but Gwen pauses beside a humming black machine with a glass top that glows softly—a 3D printer. She looks through the glass into the main chamber and sees something that looks like a bike helmet.

"Early design for an interface cap," Evelyn says.

"Has it been tested?" Gwen asks as the mechanism slowly prints another microscopic layer of carbon fiber.

"Only with a few miners so far. But when they're wearing the cap, they're able to process about twenty percent more data than the hourly average."

Gwen shrugs, unimpressed. "It's not about speed or quantity. There's more to it than that."

"That's what I've been trying to tell them," Evelyn says, tapping the glass. "But you know how it goes. Washington likes shiny objects they can sell to Congress and the taxpayer."

Next to the printer, Gwen recognizes a few of the portable arrays like the one she used during her test to be Rosemary Martin's miner. They're lined up on a workbench, above which is a pegboard holding a dozen of the dark metallic rings used during the tethering procedure.

Evelyn follows her gaze. "Now these portables, they're actually a good investment. They'll be universal within the year. At least for people in the field. You guys at the Watergate will stick with the Series Tens."

"I'm not going back there," Gwen says, taking one of the rings off the board. "No chance."

"Let's not worry about that right now."

"These new?" Gwen asks, turning the ring over in her hands and testing its weight.

"It's lighter, but functions the same," Evelyn says. "The only real difference is these only require a few drops of the miner's blood instead of a full vial."

"Sounds great to me," Gwen says. She puts the ring back on its peg and follows Evelyn through a door to the front of the building.

Unlike the packed warehouse, this space is open and airy. Offices and huddle rooms surround a common area occupied by couches, beanbag chairs, a cappuccino station, and a Ping-Pong table. It's the epitome of a hip and modern think-tank operation. But Gwen's eyes are drawn to the large windows that look out into darkness. She feels suddenly exposed.

"We're not staying in here, are we?"

"No, this is design and manufacturing," Evelyn says. "Active arrays are downstairs."

They go through a door situated behind the reception desk—after Evelyn goes through the full procedure with the security scanner—and take a set of stairs heading down.

"This facility houses one of the main server banks for the East Coast," Evelyn says. "So you'll have direct access to the system."

As they descend, the air gets progressively colder. By the time they reach the bottom of the steps, Gwen's shivering. "Holy shit," she says, folding her arms tight across her chest, her T-shirt providing little protection.

Evelyn chuckles. "You think this is cold, you should feel it inside the server room. But don't worry. We come prepared." She opens a door right next to the steps, revealing a closetful of puffer jackets, half of which are solid red, the others solid blue.

"Team colors?" Gwen asks.

"Sort of," Evelyn says. "It's a reference to *The Matrix*. You know . . . red pill or blue pill?"

Gwen takes a red one. A nametag with *Dozer Poser* is pinned to the front. She puts it on, zips up—feeling warmer instantly—and thrusts her chilled hands in the pockets, where she finds a pack of Marlboro Reds and a half container of orange Tic Tacs. Realizing that she hasn't eaten anything substantial since lunch more than twelve hours ago, she downs the entire thing of Tic Tacs in one go.

Evelyn laughs. "Orange pill for you, I guess."

"You're not going to put on a jacket?" asks Gwen.

"Nah, I've got my trusty hot flashes to keep me warm."

Three Series Ten arrays are positioned side by side in the center of the room, their thick fiber-optic cables feeding up into the ceiling. Just beyond them is a heavy glass door, the server room visible behind it.

Gwen chooses the center array, sits down, and touches her hand to the reflective surface. As the monitors fan out, an arrow appears, directing her to the blood draw port. She places her finger on the port and seconds later the cable from her array lights up, casting a warm, pink-orange glow in the frigid space.

The Harvester interface appears on the main screen.

"I've been meaning to ask about this," Gwen says, pointing to Suki Hammamoto's amber-colored icon. "All my past subjects' icons disappeared when I got untethered from them. Why is hers still here?"

"Oh, the two of you are untethered, that's why it's amber," Evelyn says. "Her data's not archived yet, is all. As soon as data management gets its act together, she'll be removed from the system. Until then the icon has to sit in someone's queue, may as well be yours. It'll be gone soon enough."

Gwen nods and taps the green icon next to Suki's, which opens Rosemary Martin's data stream. Her last analysis from the predictive PCR algorithm pops to the forefront.

"You gonna broadcast?" Evelyn asks.

"Yeah," Gwen says. "I want people to see this."

She lets out a steady breath, initiates the broadcast, and begins to dig through the information.

Evelyn watches over her shoulder. "What prompted you to run this search?"

"The senator had some sort of virus or bacteria in her gut, and I wanted to be sure it wasn't something serious," Gwen says, pointing to a list on one of the side screens. "I found out that it was just a common strand of *Listeria*. But in addition to the *Listeria* protein fragments, I found a few DNA strand breaks."

"What kind?" Evelyn says, eyeing a chart on a side monitor.

"Mostly single-strand, I think. I didn't get that far before shit went sideways at the Watergate."

"She being treated for cancer?"

Gwen enters a few commands into the system, slowly at first and then more rapidly as her fingers warm up. "Doesn't look like it. She's not currently receiving chemotherapy or radiation. Maybe in the past?"

"Accessing all of her old medical records will take a lot of time," Evelyn says.

"That's why I'm gonna run a next-gen sequence instead. That'll show us if she's got any cancer markers."

Window upon window of data appears on the main screen, and Gwen swipes them all over to the side monitors after a cursory glance. After a minute or so, she pauses, nods vigorously, and enlarges a multi-columned table.

"What have you got?"

"Biomarker analysis came back clean," Gwen says. "No known genetic mutations that would indicate cancer."

"So the breaks must be from some sort of environmental exposure."

"Right. But where in the hell would she have encountered something toxic enough to damage her DNA?"

"Anything out of the ordinary come up on the PCR?"

Gwen reloads the table of proteins she used to pinpoint the *Listeria* infection. "Let's see . . ." she says, scanning the data. "She's got antibodies for influenza, COVID, chicken pox, all the common shit."

"What's that?" Evelyn says, pointing.

"It looks like . . . wait, that's weird," Gwen says. She enters a few search terms and scans the results. "It's a protein fragment for a strain of *Hantavirus*."

Before she can dig any further, muffled voices sound from the direction of the stairwell, and Gwen and Evelyn freeze for a long moment before Evelyn grabs Gwen's arm and pulls her away from the array. Gwen resists at first, pointing to the table on the screen, certain it contains the answers she's been after, but Evelyn yanks her arm hard, forcing her to go with her to the server room.

The glass door slides open at the press of a button. A blast of cold air hits the two women in the face as they rush in, and the door hisses closed again behind them.

"Could it be security?" Gwen whispers.

Evelyn shakes her head silently as she leads the way through rows of server racks, desperate to put as much distance as possible between themselves and whoever else is inside the building. The racks holding the super-cooled drives are tall enough to prevent them from being seen from the other room.

They're still working their way to the back when three loud bangs sound from above.

The hum from the servers and glass enclosure muffles the sound, but the noise is unmistakable.

Gunshots.

"He found me," Gwen says. "Is there another way out of here?"

"There's a door at the back that will take us to a service elevator. It goes up to the loading dock where we came in."

"If we get on that elevator and someone's up there waiting for us, we're fucked," Gwen whispers.

"What else are we going do?" Evelyn says, hugging her chest to fight off the frigid air and probably a healthy dose of fear.

There's a quick blast of radio static somewhere nearby, followed by a male voice. Gwen and Evelyn stare at each other with wide eyes.

Someone's inside the server room with them.

There's no other choice, Gwen thinks as she grabs Evelyn's hand and they rush toward the back door, Gwen's injured knee starting to protest again. But as they approach the door, Gwen sees a sign on the wall that stops her dead in her tracks.

Vacuum suppression system will engage and seal this room in the event of a fire or aerosolized contaminant.

She yanks Evelyn to one side, behind a server rack. "Wait," she whispers.

"What are you doing?" Evelyn whispers back, eyes darting between Gwen and the back door.

Gwen reaches into her jacket pocket and takes out the pack of Marlboros. Tucked into the cellophane wrapper is a book of matches.

"Go out the door and hit the button for the elevator," she whispers into Evelyn's ear. "But as soon as you hit it, get back here to me. Okay?"

Another burst of static, closer than before.

Gwen rips off a match, holds it up to Evelyn, and points at the sign. It only takes a few seconds before Evelyn gets it. She nods enthusiastically, letting Gwen know she understands the plan.

Go, Gwen mouths, and sets the tip of the match against the striker on the matchbook.

Evelyn hurries to the exit door. She hits a red button, and the door slides open with a slight *whoosh*. The service elevator is almost directly outside, and she hits the button to call the elevator and is back in the server room in an instant.

A voice shouts at the sound of the elevator descending.

Gwen strikes the match, and the flame sputters to life in the icy air. She holds the flame to the rest of the matchbook, sparking the remaining matches, then opens one of the server doors and puts the flaming book down at the base of the cabinet. She shakes out a few cigarettes, sets them next to the small fire along with the pack, and then watches as the cellophane shrinks and melts, and the paper carton begins to blacken.

"Now," she whispers.

They move silently around the perimeter of the server room toward the glass door they entered through, pausing only once when they hear running footsteps a few rows over. Once the footsteps pass, Evelyn and Gwen break into a sprint. They reach the door, hit the button to open it, and run back into the space with the arrays.

Seconds later, an alarm rings out. Behind them, they hear the metallic clang of the server room locks engaging, followed by the roar of a massive vacuum.

As they run past the arrays, Gwen turns her head to look at the one she was working on. Someone has cut all the fiber-optic cables, leaving the severed ends dangling from the ceiling.

They reach the base of the stairs, but are forced to stop short when they hear someone coming down from above. Evelyn shoves Gwen into the closet with the jackets, then follows her inside and quietly shuts the door.

They hear voices through the door. The man who came down the stairs is apparently using a walkie-talkie, and several frantic voices are coming through. The man shouts that he's coming and runs in the direction of the server room.

Gwen and Evelyn slip out of the closet, and Gwen looks toward the server room. A man dressed all in black and wearing a ski mask is pounding on the heavy glass door, which is now locked. On the other side of the glass, a man and a woman dressed in similar fashion have their guns drawn. They wave their colleague aside and start firing at the glass door.

Evelyn and Gwen dash up the steps.

The door at the top of the stairs now has a gaping hole where the knob and locking mechanism once were. They push through it, then sprint through the open area and back into the warehouse. Gwen's knee is on fire, but she refuses to let it slow her down. The steel garage door at the loading dock is still closed, but the door next to it has been smashed open. Evelyn races toward it, but Gwen veers toward the workbench next to the 3D printer.

"Gwen, let's go!"

"Hold on!" Gwen reaches the workbench, grabs one of the portable arrays and a tethering ring, then turns and races toward the loading dock. Evelyn is waiting for her by the door, and together they dash outside.

A black SUV is parked behind their car, blocking them in, but Evelyn gets behind the wheel anyway. "Come on, hurry!" she screams, slamming the door shut and firing up the engine. Gwen gets inside with her cargo, and Evelyn has the car in reverse even before Gwen's door is closed.

The back bumper smashes into the side of the SUV, rocking it back a few inches.

Evelyn pulls forward and then guns it backward again, moving the SUV even further this time.

She repeats this maneuver twice more, then cuts the wheel hard and swings the car around enough to pull out of the parking spot, scraping the front bumper against the concrete loading dock as they complete the turn.

Evelyn smashes the gas pedal, and the car jumps forward—but not before a bullet rips through Gwen's shoulder, sending a spray of blood all over the inside of the windshield.

With a shriek, Gwen grabs at her shoulder. She looks back at the loading dock and sees the three black-clad figures getting into the damaged SUV.

"Hold on!" Evelyn shouts as the car jumps over the first speed bump. She doesn't slow for any of the others either. She cuts the wheel hard as they reach the gatehouse, barrels right through the wooden barrier arms, and skids onto the street.

As they accelerate away from the industrial park, Gwen carefully wriggles her injured arm out of the jacket sleeve and clamps her hand over the wound. After a few deep breaths, she peeks at her arm and watches the blood well from the hole in her deltoid.

"Is it bad?" Evelyn asks.

"Hurts like a bitch, but it missed the bone, I think."

Evelyn tears through a red light and screeches around a sharp turn. "Good. I'm going to let you out."

"What? No!"

"Gwen, listen to me," Evelyn says. She nods to the portable array and tethering ring wedged next to Gwen's thigh. "Take those and find a way to get online. I'll lead them away."

"Evelyn, no! I can't let you do that."

"You don't have a choice, Gwen. These people aren't trying to make you stop anymore. They want you *dead*. This is the only way." She slams on the brakes, and the car fishtails and screeches to a stop. "Go!" she screams.

Gwen bends her arm back into the jacket sleeve with a whimper, takes the portable array and tethering ring, and gets out of the car. The second she shuts the door behind her, the car lurches forward and speeds off, its one working taillight disappearing up the road.

Gwen sees that she's in a residential neighborhood but doesn't have time to take in the details. She only barely manages to duck behind a hedgerow, holding the portable array to her chest, before the black SUV comes flying around the corner and roars past. When it's gone, she looks around for someplace to hide.

She's in someone's yard, in front of a small, weathered house, the lights off. It's not even clear if it's currently lived in. Gwen moves around to the side of the house and sees exactly what she needs.

There's a shed in the back yard.

She hobbles over to it, desperate to get out of the open.

Just as she reaches the door, an explosion stops her in her tracks.

Seconds later, a fireball blooms in the distance.

CHAPTER
TWENTY

SPENCER WATCHES THE CAR BURN. Its hood and windshield are crushed beneath the main body of a tractor-trailer. It looks as though it drove straight into the side of the truck, traveling fast enough to effectively wedge itself underneath. The truck's cab door is open, and the truck driver is nowhere to be seen. Perhaps he's injured, or stumbled away to pull out his phone. Spencer doesn't care as long as he's gone.

"There's no way they survived that crash," Spencer's man says, turning around in his seat and looking at the woman in the back for support.

"He's right, we're done here," she chimes in, leaning forward between the front seats and grabbing Spencer's arm. "Let's go."

Spencer whips his arm free of her grasp, kicks open the crumpled passenger-side door, and gets out, ignoring the protests from his team. The heat is intense as he walks toward the car, and he has to shield his face. He moves toward the car at an angle, avoiding a puddle of flaming fluid, hoping to get a glimpse at the interior, but thick black smoke and flames obscure his view. He gets closer still, but when part of the truck's side peels away and crashes down on the car's roof, sending a shower of sparks and a plume of heat outward, he's forced to back away. Cardboard boxes spill out of the truck and onto the flaming vehicle, adding literal fuel to the fire.

In the distance, he hears the first sirens.

"Spencer, come on!" his man yells from the SUV.

With a final glance into the flames, Spencer jogs back to the SUV, gets in, and leaves the wreck behind.

WHEN THEY GET BACK to the garage, Rosemary and the others are gathered around a laptop watching news chopper footage of the accident. Police and EMS workers stand at a distance from the conflagration as firefighters snake a hose from a pumper truck to a nearby hydrant.

Spencer joins them and watches for a few seconds before he pulls Rosemary to the side.

"Are you okay?" she asks.

"I'm fine. We're all fine," he says, glancing over at his team. "At the facility, I saw she had been broadcasting again. Did she find anything?"

"Nothing conclusive," Rosemary says. "And it all can be explained away."

He breathes a deep sigh of relief. "Have you talked to Mr. Seanwoo?"

Rosemary winces and gives his hand a quick squeeze. "He's angry it came to this. He made that *very* clear."

Spencer knows there will be questions once the dust settles— tough questions for which he doesn't have a lot of good answers. But at least the operation is still on track. It won't be pretty, but he can handle the fallout from above. He's done it before.

"When word reaches the presidential committee that Gwen Elliott is dead, they're gonna jump all over the situation," he says. "The Watergate, the research facility, the boyfriend. They're going to turn this thing upside down looking for answers."

"I know. But I think we can turn it into an advantage," Rosemary says with a wry smile.

"How?" he asks, suddenly very curious.

"We implicate the woman, Evelyn Young." She points to Maria, who's sitting on a folding chair in the corner, chunky headphones over her ears and a computer on her lap. "Maria's already creating a suspicious trail that leads right to her email and social channels."

"From where?"

"Russia, where else?" Rosemary says. "It'll be just another in a long line of Russian efforts to fuck with an American election."

Spencer nods slowly, his admiration growing. "That could work," he says. "What'd boss man have to say about it?"

"He has a lot of faith in Maria's skills, so he gave us the green light. You know, I had my reservations about her at first, but I've come around. She's a real asset."

Maria must somehow sense she's the topic of conversation, because she looks up from her screen and gives them both a quick middle finger before getting back to work.

"You should go," Spencer says, resting his palm on the small of Rosemary's back and giving it a short rub.

"I wish you could come with me."

"Me too," he says.

He turns to go. But Rosemary takes his hand and leads him away from the others. Once they're out of sight, she kisses him on his cheeks and lips and holds him tight.

"You saved me, Spencer. Thank you."

He wraps his arms around her and buries his face in her neck, breathing in the scent of her.

"So you can save the rest of us."

CHAPTER
TWENTY-ONE

GWEN STARES at the black cloud rising over the roofs of the neighborhood, a dark billowing mass peppered with orange and yellow sparks flitting around like fireflies. *Please don't let it be her,* she thinks, but a pit opens in her gut. She wants to run toward it, sprint to where her friend could be hurt or worse, but her legs won't move. Despite the red jacket she borrowed from the Harvester facility, she begins to shiver. She can't tell if it's the damp night air, blood loss from the gunshot wound in her shoulder, or her rising anger and sadness and fear.

She ducks into the shed and closes the door behind her. A switch inside the door illuminates a single bulb in the ceiling, its glass coated in dust and cobwebs. In the dim glow, she finds a hoarder's delight. One side of the shed is piled high with terra cotta pots, bags of fertilizer, dirt, grass seed, and an armamentarium of garden tools and machine parts. The opposite side is dominated by heavy wooden shelving stacked with moldy cardboard boxes and dirty plastic totes. In between, a dusty riding mower that looks like it hasn't moved since the combustion engine was invented takes up nearly every inch of free space. Beyond it is a workbench with a metal stool, books stacked on the seat.

After a few attempts at skirting around the mower, at one

point nearly dropping the portable array, Gwen gives up and decides to climb over it. She steps on the nearly flat back tire, shimmies past the seat and steering wheel, and slides down the hood to the workbench, leaving a streak in the dust.

Clamped to one of the wooden studs above the bench is a metal work light. She twists its switch and is surprised when it turns on, casting a bright pool of light on the bench's surface. After pushing aside boxes and coffee tins of nails, bolts, and screws, she sets down the portable array. She wants to activate it right away, get back to her data, and expose whatever secrets are hidden inside, but first needs to find something for her wounded shoulder.

She pulls open a few drawers and finds a hardware store's worth of crap inside. But after some digging, she uncovers a pile of neatly folded rags. She picks out the cleanest-looking one in the stack, slides her blood-streaked arm out of the jacket sleeve, and puts the rag on her injury, wincing as she presses on the wound.

For a moment she just holds the rag there, eyes closed, trying to catch her breath. When the world finally settles again, she grabs a roll of electrical tape hanging on a nail near the shop light. She uses her thumbnail to find the edge, bites down on the newly exposed flap, and pulls out a long strip. Sticking the end to her upper bicep, she winds the tape around the rag, securing it to her shoulder, then rips the end off with her teeth. Now that both hands are finally free, she grabs another rag, wipes the bloody smudges off the surface of the portable array, and clears away as much sawdust and grime from the surface of the bench as she can. Finally she knocks the stack of books off the stool and takes a seat.

"Time to end this," she says, pulling the jacket around her but leaving her injured arm out of the sleeve.

She touches the surface of the device, and the blood draw tray slides out. She sets her index finger on the tray, feels it extract its sample, then lets out a long breath as the tray retracts and the entire device begins to hum. Seconds later, the laser keyboard projection streams from the device onto the pocked and rutted surface of the workbench, and the Harvester interface glows before her. But instead of the home page, a dialog box is centered on the projected screen, informing Gwen that she's not online.

She searches for Wi-Fi signals, but the ones in range all require passwords. A hotspot is available from the region's largest internet service provider, but she's not a subscriber; the job has always taken care of her internet needs.

Then she remembers that Darnell has an account. She has no idea whether it will even work, but she's out of options.

She enters Darnell's email address in the username box, then tabs to the password box. Tears blur her vision as she tries to remember what Darnell told her when they were lying in bed after the first time they made love. She wanted to check her email before going to sleep, so he'd given her his password.

Of course I did that to him instead of just enjoying the moment, she thinks, pounding the workbench with her fist.

She types something. It doesn't work.

Tries again with the same result.

She's in the middle of guess number three when the shed door flies open.

"Who's in there?" a man yells, holding a shotgun.

"Don't shoot!" Gwen says, throwing her hands in the air. Pain stabs through her shoulder, the electrical tape pulling at her skin as her arm goes up and the jacket falls away. She lets out a strangled cry but doesn't lower her arms.

For a few seconds, staring down the barrel of the man's gun, she thinks that maybe this is the man who's been chasing her—until she realizes that he's wearing pajamas and slippers. Tufts of white hair poke out of the shirt near his collar, matching the wisps whipping around his head.

"I'm not stealing anything, I swear," she says. "It's an emergency."

He lowers his gun a few inches, a confused expression on his face. "Whaddaya got there?" he says, using the barrel to point at the glowing array.

"It's just a computer," she says, shifting aside so he can see. "I have to do something urgent, that's why I'm in here."

He lowers the gun to his side. "You're hurt."

Gwen slowly lowers her hands and grabs at the rag, the brittle electrical tape coming loose. She nods, but the choked sob that escapes from deep inside says it all.

"You're in some kind of trouble, ain't ya, honey?" he says, setting his gun on the inside of the door next to a garden trowel. He walks to the back of the mower and waves her toward him. "Come on, let's get you fixed up."

The old man shoves a few of the boxes around to clear a path past the mower. "I gotta get this place organized," he says, pushing one last box to reach Gwen. He holds out a hand for her, but she doesn't take it.

"It's okay," he says, a gentle smile on his stubbly face. "You grab that thing of yours and we'll go inside and take care of your shoulder. My Ruthie was a nurse, and the medicine cabinets are still packed to the gills."

"Thank you," she says, wiping away tears and smiling back at him.

"I don't know a computer from a blender," he says. "But that looks like a good one."

"We'll see," Gwen says as she takes the man's hand.

HE INTRODUCES HIMSELF AS OLIVER, clears a spot for her at the kitchen table, then goes off in search of first aid supplies. From what Gwen can see, he uses the same organizational strategy in the house as in the shed. Dishes, pots, pans, cans, bottles, and boxes clutter nearly every surface. The place smells like a combination of cinnamon and onions, which inexplicably makes her stomach growl. She checks her pocket for the tethering ring, then drapes the jacket over the back of one of the chairs and sits down at the table, setting the portable array in front of her.

"Oliver, do you have Wi-Fi?" she yells.

He comes back into the kitchen and dumps boxes of gauze, rolls of white tape, a brown bottle of hydrogen peroxide, a clear bottle of alcohol, and a few tubes of various creams and ointments on the chair next to her.

"I just brought a bunch of stuff," he says, distracted by the device sitting on his table next to a stack of empty Tupperware containers. "Wow, look at that."

"Do you have Wi-Fi?" she asks again.

"Yeah, my granddaughter set it up for me last Christmas after she bought me one of those iPads," he says. "She's out in Colorado, so it's the only way I get to see my great-grandbabies."

"Which one is it?" Gwen says, pointing to the list on her screen.

Oliver leans in, squints, then points to the third one down. "That's the one," he says. "I don't remember the password, but I've got it written down in my book. Hold on."

As Oliver goes in search of the password, Gwen grabs the bottle of alcohol and heads to the sink. She picks off the remnants of the electrical tape and slowly peels back the rag. The bullet wound looks angry, rimmed in red. She pulls up her ruined short sleeve and leans forward over a stack of dirty dishes, the congealed food and grease doing a great job of curbing her hunger. She pours alcohol over the wound, working hard to stifle a scream, then cups her hand and pours some into her palm. She sets the bottle aside, takes a few deep breaths, and works the remaining alcohol into the raw flesh with her fingers. She has to hold onto the sink afterwards as stars dance in front of her eyes.

Next to the sink is a paper towel holder. She yanks a long sheet of towels from the roll and holds them to her shoulder, as blood is once again flowing freely. When she feels steady enough, she makes her way back to the table.

"Here you go," Oliver says, coming back into the kitchen with a yellow stickie note. He stops when he sees her holding the paper towels to her shoulder. "Are you okay?"

"I'm fine. I just cleaned the wound is all."

"I was gonna do that for you." He drops the note on the table and moves her hand and the paper towels aside so he can look at her shoulder.

"I managed," she says, grabbing the stickie note. But when she goes to type the password into the box, he keeps hold of her arm, studying the wound.

"Bullet went right through, huh? That's lucky," he says, gently probing around the edges. "Good thing it missed all the important stuff."

"How can you tell?" Gwen asks, punching in the password with her free hand.

"I saw my share of close calls in the army," Oliver says.

He grabs one of the tubes of cream and squeezes a large dollop onto Gwen's wound, then puts some more onto one of the gauze pads. Gwen watches as the Harvester interface loads, struggling on Oliver's tepid Wi-Fi.

"Thank you for helping me," she says.

"Don't have it in me to do anything less," he says. "Especially for a damsel in distress. And from the looks of it, you're *definitely* into something serious. You should probably talk to the authorities."

He puts the gauze in place and makes her hold it there while he rips off a length of surgical tape. He wraps it around the gauze, apologizing as she sucks in a quick breath against the pain. After a few more strips of tape, he gives the bandage a pat, wipes the dried blood from her bicep and forearm with an alcohol-moistened pack of gauze, then lets Gwen have her arm back.

"I need to do something first," she says, pointing at the glowing screen, "and then I'm going straight to the cops. I promise."

As Oliver gathers his things up, the screen finishes loading, and Gwen sees the analysis she and Evelyn were studying at the research facility before everything went to hell. The weird *Hantavirus* protein fragment is still highlighted in yellow. She initiates the broadcast, clicks on the odd bit of protein found in Rosemary's blood, and conducts a search for places where the strain in question is endemic. A spinning wheel appears as the system chugs along.

"You do what you've gotta do," Oliver says, heading toward the stove. "In the meantime, how about tea or coffee? I've got both."

"Tea would be great, thanks," Gwen says, watching a blank table slowly fill with data.

"I don't mean to pry, but are you one of them hackers?" he says, filling a kettle with water from the sink. "Not the bad kind, of course. You don't seem like that to me."

"I'm a data miner," Gwen says, smiling at Oliver to reassure him. "One of the good guys."

"If you say so," he says after a pause, doing a bad job of masking the disappointment in his voice.

"I can't tell you too much about what I'm doing, but I promise you it's really important," Gwen says. "And when this is all over, people are going to thank you for helping me."

He sets the kettle on the burner and turns around. "No, that's okay. I don't want anything to do with any of this stuff." He waves his hands around his head like he's shooing a fly.

"What's wrong?" Gwen says, turning aside from the Harvester screen to look at him.

"Look," he says. "I probably got no place even having an opinion about what you smart people are up to. And I think folks should just keep their mouths shut when they don't know what they're talking about." But apparently that's not what he intends to do on this particular occasion, as he continues. "Ruthie and I were both military brats. We met on a base where both our dads were serving, and we got married young. Her dad died a few years later in Korea, which made her awful nervous when my number for Vietnam came up. And I had a couple close scrapes too, I'll tell ya. But I made it through, thank God."

"That must have been tough on you both," Gwen says, making

sure to stay with him. "But what does this have to do with me?"

"Well, you see, Ruthie's pop died, and I got real close myself. And both of us were fighting against an enemy who, you know, among lots of other bad things, thought it was their right to watch over their people. That's all," he says. "Now I hear on the television all the time how what you people are doing is different. But, you know, it's just hard for me to shake how much it feels like what we fought against in those wars."

Gwen nods. "That's fair," she says. "But you're talking about communist governments. This isn't the same. We aren't in the business of watching *everyone*. We use this system to monitor only those people in position to affect a lot of others, because even honest people can make mistakes. So I do my job for the good of everyone, including the people I'm assigned to watch over. Does that make sense?"

The kettle starts to whistle.

"Yeah, that's how it always starts," Oliver says with a shrug, taking the kettle off the burner. "But like I said, what do I know?"

Just then, the system beeps with the search results. Gwen looks at the regions listed and sees that *Hantavirus* is most prevalent in Asia. As she leans forward to examine the list further, Oliver hands her a steaming *World's Greatest Pop-Pop* mug.

"This is weird," she says, barely glancing at the mug as she takes it from Oliver.

"Sorry, all I got is Earl Grey."

"No, not the . . . thank you. This is perfect," she says. "It turns out that this person here was once infected by a virus from Asia. I'm surprised, that's all."

"Oh, honey, let me tell you," Oliver says, blowing across the lip of his own mug. "They got some nasty ones over there. You wouldn't believe the crud I picked up during my two tours. Once I was stationed in Saigon . . ."

But Gwen doesn't hear the rest of his story as she taps away at the glowing keyboard on Oliver's kitchen table, her fingers a blur in the laser light.

SPENCER GLANCES at the chamber to make sure it's empty, then places his gun and magazine in their designated spots inside the case, alongside a pair of handcuffs and a butterfly knife. Once they're secured in the foam, he shuts the lid and flips the latches closed. A sense of calm washes over him as he exhales the breath it feels like he's been holding since discovering Gwen Elliott's identity.

Too bad we couldn't get her to play ball. That would have been so much easier.

"She's back online!" Maria shouts from across the room.

Spencer is dumbstruck.

No, this has to be over, he thinks, but he knows it isn't by the way Maria is suddenly pacing back and forth behind her laptop and wringing her hands.

"Are you sure?" he says, sprinting over and skidding to a stop next to her.

"It's definitely her," Maria says, pointing to the computer. "She's right back where she left off a few hours ago."

Spencer angles the screen so he can see it. A table appears detailing antibodies for all the viruses Rosemary has ever encountered—a map of a lifetime of illnesses and sick days, cold medicines and chicken soup, vaccinations and doctors' visits. A plethora of avenues to explore, should one choose to pursue them.

And he knows Gwen Elliott will. That's what makes her dangerous.

He slides his phone out of his pocket.

"Good, you're calling him?" Maria asks.

"Not yet," he says, taking a few steps away.

"They're going to see the broadcast, Spencer! You can't hide this!"

"Don't you think I know that?" he screams, spinning around on Maria and pointing at her computer. "Find her!"

Maria looks like she's about to start yelling again, but then sits down at the laptop with a heavy sigh. Spencer turns his back to her and dials.

"Bring her back," he says the instant his man picks up.

"But sir . . ."

"Right now!" Spencer screams, then ends the call.

He paces around the room, searching for a different way forward, desperate to avoid what's coming. But he knows he can't. Maria's right. There will be expectations, and his only choice is to meet them.

There's no other way.

He checks his watch. It'll be dawn soon. *The press will be ravenous*, he thinks. *And I'm about to throw them red meat.*

He walks over to Maria and looks over her shoulder at her screen. "What's she doing?"

"I'm not really sure," Maria says, toggling between several windows. "I'm trying to follow where she's going with these searches, but like I've told you, she does things differently than any other miner I've ever seen."

He points to a highlighted row showing *Hantavirus* among the protein fragments found in Rosemary's blood. "Why is she focused on this one?"

"I don't know," Maria says, pointing to a world map on her screen. "She's already found that this virus—or at least the variant the senator encountered—isn't common around here, which obviously isn't good."

"This seems really slow," he says, pointing at a table where the rows are sporadically filling with numbers. "Am I wrong?"

"No, I noticed that too. Her analyses are usually a blur. My guess is she's on a severely throttled connection to the Harvester network—maybe even using a commercial entry point. I'm running an algorithm to try and pinpoint a location, but the system's firewalls are really thick."

Maria maximizes one of Gwen's windows as the data field changes from blood and DNA analyses to a scan of Rosemary's lungs.

"What the hell is she after now?" Spencer says.

"Looks like she's fishing around the respiratory tract. Which doesn't make sense since she's already singled out *Hanta*. She shouldn't need additional confirmation that it's a pulmonary virus."

Realization dawns on him. "I don't think she's trying to confirm the 'what.' She's trying to figure out the 'where.'

Just then the garage door begins to open, the gears squealing in protest, and the SUV that left only minutes prior pulls back into the garage. Spencer walks back to the table with his gun case and flips open the latches. But instead of the gun, he grabs the butterfly knife. He flicks it open and heads straight for the SUV.

The back door swings open and Rosemary gets out, a look of confusion etched in her features at the sight of Spencer charging toward her.

That confusion only grows when he grabs her wrist, pulls her arm toward him . . .

And slices across her Harvester tattoo.

PULMONARY ANALYSIS COMPLETE. Exposure to foreign air pollutants confirmed. Bilateral infiltrates of the subject's lung parenchyma are consistent with—

The screen blinks. Gwen's data analysis disappears, and in its place is the Harvester home page. The screen shows two icons, one for Suki Hammamoto and the other for Rosemary Martin, but now *both* are amber in color. Hovering above them is a dialog box that says, *Data miner has no active subjects,* and a countdown runs backward from 5 . . .

4 . . .

3 . . .

2 . . .

1 . . .

The device goes dark.

Gwen reaches out and touches the surface of the portable array, but nothing happens. She tries with each hand, then touches both palms to the device simultaneously, trying to elicit some sort of response, trigger it to release the blood draw port and let her log back on. Nothing works. She's shut out.

"Your computer break down?" Oliver asks from across the kitchen. He's cooking scrambled eggs, the dawn light sneaking through the small kitchen window next to the stove and casting him in a golden glow.

"I don't know," Gwen says, stunned, rubbing red lines in her forehead as she processes what just happened. "This has never happened to me before."

"Can you call tech support or something?"

"I wish it were that easy."

She stares at the dormant array, no more useful to her now than any of the other objects cluttering Oliver's kitchen table. Waves of despair crash over her, threatening to drag her under. She's so close to ending it, to discovering the secret. She knows the answer is right there, waiting—a few keystrokes, another search or two, and this will all be over.

She closes her eyes and tries to see the rest of the pulmonary analysis message, hoping her subconscious can surface it. Praying her brain can somehow draw it out if she concentrates hard enough.

What did it say?

What kind of pollutants?

Where did they come from?

The pop of the toaster makes her jump.

Oliver puts two thick slices of toast on a cracked bread plate and walks over to the table. "Eggs'll be a minute," he says, setting the plate next to Gwen. "Want some coffee?"

Gwen shakes her head, barely hearing the question. "A few more minutes," she says to herself. "That's all it would have taken."

Oliver turns off the burner, grabs the skillet in one hand and two plates in his other, and heads back to Gwen. She takes a plate from him and watches as he piles steaming eggs onto it, giving her the larger of the two helpings.

"Eat up, honey. You'll feel better."

As she reaches for her fork, a twinge of pain shoots down her arm from the bullet wound in her shoulder. She switches hands and digs into her breakfast. *No active subjects*, she thinks as she chews. *How is that possible?*

Oliver sits down next to her and maybe even says something, but she can't be sure. She shovels forkfuls of the buttery, delicious eggs into her mouth as she stares at the black cylinder, weighing the possibilities.

She needs information.

She looks around the room and notices an old Trinitron sitting atop a corner shelf opposite the kitchen table.

"Does that work?" she says, pointing at the television with an eggy fork.

"Sure does. That's why I haven't gotten one of those flat ones yet." Oliver nods to a pile of newspapers. "Clicker's probably under there somewhere."

Gwen finds the remote next to an open box of Good & Plenty. She hits the red power button and keys in the channel number for CNN even before the screen comes alive. The glowing green numbers in the corner of the screen say it's just after six a.m.

". . . *top story is the suspected terrorist attack on the Watergate facility in Washington, DC. We're still getting details this morning, but what we know so far is that sometime after ten p.m. last night a drone or some other type of remote-operated vehicle flew into the Watergate lobby and exploded, causing a fire, significant damage, and several fatalities. White House officials have told CNN that no one has yet claimed responsibility for the attack. For more on this story, we'll turn to —*"

"This involves you, doesn't it," Oliver says, his eyes wide as he watches the slightly askew image of a reporter standing on the White House lawn.

"I'm afraid so," Gwen says.

They watch snippets of broadcasts on different channels while they finish their breakfast. Oliver eyes her warily the whole time. She can't tell if he's worried or if he just wants her gone now that he knows what she's involved in. But then she lands on a local station showing the burned-out remains of Darnell's restaurant. The chyron

"Suspected Arsonist Found Dead" is emblazoned above a video of someone wheeling away an enshrouded figure on a gurney. Gwen can't hold back the sudden tears, an upwelling of emotion and adrenaline that threatens to overwhelm her. When ragged sobs erupt from deep inside her, Oliver's there like some wizened angel of mercy.

"You're in some big-time shit, ain't ya, honey?"

"I can't let them get away with this," Gwen says, pointing at the screen. "They killed him. The people who shot me. They murdered my boyfriend and they're covering it up, just like they'll cover up everything else if I don't stop them."

"It's gonna be all right," Oliver says, reaching for a stack of fast-food napkins and handing them to her. But he must sense she needs something more and pulls her toward him. She hugs him tight and doesn't let go for a long time.

"Come on, it's time to get you some real help," he says when she finally quiets down. "I'll drive you to the police station."

Gwen's wrung out, exhausted, defeated. Resignation washes over her. *It's time.*

As she reaches for the portable array, the news switches to a panel of talking heads discussing the threat that data mining poses to democracy. She barely pays attention to the familiar blather as she puts on Poser Dozer's red jacket, now with a bullet hole in the sleeve. But then she glances at the television and sees footage of Suki Hammamoto and her daughter being mobbed at Boston Logan airport playing behind the commentators.

Suki scoops up her daughter.

Pushes through the crowd, looking for an escape.

Angry faces pursue them.

Gwen's hand drifts to the jacket pocket with the tethering ring she took from the facility. She fingers the smooth surface. And as she stares at the little girl's frightened face, an idea blooms in her mind.

Oliver's right. She needs help.

And she knows where she's going to get it.

She turns to Oliver. "I'm not going to the cops," she says.

He meets her gaze with one of the most genuine looks of concern for her she's ever seen in another person. "Oh, but honey. You can't do this alone anymore."

Her heart swells as she puts a hand on his cheek. "You're right," she says. "Can I borrow your car?"

CHAPTER
TWENTY-FOUR

BLOOD WELLS between her fingers as she presses them over the long diagonal slice in her Harvester tattoo. She doesn't feel any pain—not yet. She simply stares at Spencer, stupefied by what he's just done.

He pushes her into the back of the SUV and gets in after her.

"RNC headquarters," he says to the man behind the wheel.

"Sir, do you want to—"

"Drive!" Spencer screams, slamming the back door.

"My God," Rosemary says. "What have you done?"

"This is the only way."

"How the fuck am I going to explain this?" she says, thrusting her lacerated forearm toward him, droplets of blood falling on the leather seats of the SUV.

He searches the seatback pockets and finds a stack of napkins. "Just listen to me—"

"No, you screwed us all," she says, snatching the napkins from him and pressing them to her arm. She flops her head back against the seat to gather her thoughts and fend off a wave of vertigo.

"It's okay. This will work. It'll buy us some time."

When the dizziness passes, she looks at him, sitting on the edge of the seat next to her, the blade he used to disable her Harvester still clutched in his hand, his knuckles white as he squeezes the hilt. He nods his head up and down as if doing so will make what he just said true, make everything okay again. His eyes dart between her face and bleeding arm. She knows he's waiting for her to react, and after letting his expectation build, she finally does.

She starts laughing.

"What are you doing?" he asks, his face wrinkled as she chuckles, tears springing to her eyes.

"You really think you can fix this?" she says. "Oh Spencer, honey, this is over. We're done."

His eyes go dark as he holds out the blade. "Not yet," he says. "I can still salvage this."

The laughter burns away the last vestiges of adrenaline in her system, unleashing a wave of pain emanating from her forearm and traveling up across her chest. Stars fill her vision, and sourness paints the back of her throat as her stomach twists. She takes a few ragged breaths, trying to stay calm, trying to stay present, but she can't. She's about to give in to the darkness pushing in around the edges of her vision when Spencer pulls her toward him and rests her head against his chest.

"I'm sorry," she whispers. "I wish . . . I think . . ."

"It's okay, Rose," he says, stroking her hair. "We're going to get through this. I promise."

She rests against him and waits until the world stabilizes. It's quiet and warm in the back of the SUV. She wants to let herself drift off, to give in to the rocking of the car and the beating of his heart in her ears. But then the SUV hits a bump and a jolt of pain in her arm snaps her back.

"Talk to me," she says, pushing off him and sitting back in her seat. "What are we going to do?"

"We already had plans in motion to implicate the Russians. We'll just tie it all together. The Watergate, the research facility, the woman, Evelyn Young, maybe even Gwen Elliott and the boyfriend." He's clearly formulating the plan as he speaks. "And this, too. All of it."

"I don't understand," she says, the lightheadedness coming back. She closes her eyes and takes a few deep breaths.

"Pull over!" he shouts to the driver.

"What are you doing?" she asks. She turns to look out the side window and immediately wishes she didn't when her head swims and vision narrows.

"Lie back and close your eyes," he says, helping her settle back into the seat. "Keep pressure on your arm."

Rosemary hears the car stop, gravel crunching beneath the tires. Spencer gets out of the SUV and tells his man to do the same. She wants to call to him, make him explain everything to her, convince her that everything is going to be fine and that the plan is back on track. But her eyes are so heavy. So heavy.

She drifts and fades in and out. Hears Spencer tell the driver to give him his gun.

Seconds later, three shots ring out.

Her eyes snap open and her vision tilts as she sees him lean into the car through the driver's side door.

"What did you do?"

She hears the phone dialing over the car speakers. She knows she's close to fainting and must close her eyes again. A person picks up on the fourth ring.

"911, what is your emergency?"

"A man forced me to stop my car," she hears Spencer say. "He has a gun and is coming toward us."

"Sir, where are you?"

"Send help!"

"What is your location?"

"Senator, get down!" he screams.

"Sir, who is with—"

The woman's voice cuts off.

She hears Spencer gets out of the car and come around to the back. He leans in and pushes something into her hand.

"Rose, listen to me. You're going to count to one hundred and then call 911. Can you do that?"

Her head lolls against her shoulder . . .

Until he grabs the napkins and squeezes.

Pain shoots up her arm from the wound. Her head pops up as she screams at him, eyes wide.

"Rose, are you listening?"

She just nods and takes deep breaths, waiting for the pain to subside.

"You count to one hundred and call 911. Tell them you were attacked. Say that a man pulled you out of the car and cut you, but your driver fought with him. The man fled, but he shot your driver. Do you understand?"

"You shot him?" she says. "Is he dead?"

"Yes," Spencer says. "He heard everything. I couldn't risk it. Plus, it helps with the story."

He grabs her midsection and scoots her toward the door. He swings her legs out, and she cries out when her arm bumps against the edge of the seat. He holds her steady until she nods her head to let him know she's okay, the cool night air helping keep her conscious.

"What about you?" she says. "What are you going to do?"

"I'm going to figure out how this ends."

BRIGHT AFTERNOON SUNSHINE filters through the honey locusts that line the streets of Beacon Hill, dappling the red brick sidewalks and brightly painted front doors. Flowers bloom in purples, oranges, whites, and yellows, vestiges of summer decorating window boxes and stoops in the dwindling days before autumn rolls across Massachusetts.

But the only thing decorating the home Gwen pulls up to in Oliver's Subaru is a "for sale" sign.

Inside a cloth shopping bag on the passenger's seat are the portable array, tethering ring, and a few snacks Oliver insisted she take for the trip. It took a while to convince him she'd be okay on her own, but he eventually relented and made her promise to call once she got everything sorted out. By the time she left, she felt like she'd adopted him, or he her. Either way, she was happy and thinks he was too.

She gets out, locks the car, and takes a deep breath to calm her nerves. All the blinds are drawn, and a few rolled and rubber-banded newspapers clutter the welcome mat. She briefly wonders if she's at the wrong address, until she sees the handwritten sign taped to the front door.

No press.

Gwen climbs the front steps and rings the doorbell. When no

one comes, she tries again, and then a third time before she hears a voice call out from inside the house.

"Read the sign," the woman yells from the other side of the door, her dark form barely visible through the antique frosted glass panels.

"I'm not with the press, Mrs. Hammamoto," Gwen yells. She pauses for a beat, collecting herself, dreading the next part. "My name is Gwen Elliott. I was your data miner."

She braces for outrage, imagines the door whipping open and a pissed-off, former pharmaceutical executive lunging at her with murder in her eyes. She expects screaming, cursing, tears—the kind of scene the neighbors will be talking about for years to come at summer block parties.

Instead all she gets is a muffled snort, followed by what could be best described as exasperated laughter.

"Boy, I must have really been someone once upon a time," Suki says. "You're the fourth one this week." Gwen hears a young girl calling from deeper in the house. "Just leave us alone," Suki says.

"Wait, please," Gwen says, moving closer to the door. "I'm telling you the truth. I can prove it. Your blood type is A positive. You take medication for your thyroid and anxiety."

Gwen watches Suki's shadow on the other side of the door shrink as she walks away. She tries to peer through the opaque glass but can't see Suki any longer.

"You're in perimenopause and it's giving you insomnia," she says, her lips right against the door jamb, trying to project her voice through the crack and into the house. "On days where your hormone levels fluctuate the most, you take an antihistamine at night to fall asleep, sometimes with a glass of wine."

The little girl yells for her mom again and Suki tells her to hold on, which indicates to Gwen that she's probably listening, so she keeps going.

"I know it's wine by the tannins. My guess is something red like Merlot."

"None of that proves anything," Suki says, her figure now visible again through the glass. "You could figure out all of that just by watching the broadcast of my data feed."

Gwen searches for something else, some piece of information that will prove her identity, something only she could know.

"Okay, but every Thursday morning at the same time, I'd see a spike in some of your stress biomarkers. Cortisol, alpha-amylase, chromogranin A. Things like that. It's easy to chalk that up to exercise because it's common in athletes, which I know you are. But I don't think that's it. I have a hunch it's something else."

After a pause, Gwen sees Suki approaching. Gwen steps back from the glass to not freak her out.

"Why? What makes you think that?" Suki says, her voice coming through more clearly now that she's right at the door.

"Because of what would happen right after the numbers spiked, and then because of what would sometimes happen later that day."

Suki stands there, quiet.

"About ten minutes after the stress hormones reached their peak, I'd sometimes see counter proteins hit your bloodstream, ones typically connected to people experiencing a sense of calm or relief. Not always, but most of the time. That got me wondering about the cause. So I'd watch what happened at your company to see if there was any correlation."

When Suki still doesn't say anything, Gwen quickly proceeds, afraid that she's going to walk away again.

"On the days I'd see you calming down after experiencing stress, Aevitas's stock would usually close up on the day. When I didn't see that happen, the stock price would usually stay the same or even dip a bit. So . . . I think you must have some sort of meeting or call every Thursday that's really important to you and the company. Important enough that it affects you physically."

Suki doesn't say anything, but Gwen can see she's still standing there. After a minute or so, Gwen risks a few steps forward.

"Mrs. Hammamoto, please. It's important."

Suddenly the door opens and Suki's standing there in a bathrobe and rumpled pajamas. Even though it's afternoon, her hair is a shambles as if she's just rolled out of bed.

"We had our call with the DSMB every Thursday," she says, pulling her robe closed then folding her arms across her chest, either for warmth or as a defensive maneuver.

Gwen takes a step back to give her space. "What's that?"

"Data safety monitoring board. They're the ones who watch clinical trials," she says, her dark eyes wandering over Gwen. "You'd probably like them. You guys have similar jobs."

"How's that?" Gwen asks, just to keep Suki talking, even though she knows the answer.

"They watch everything and catch every fuckup, big or small."

Gwen lets the comment hang for a few seconds, happy to absorb the jab and many more from this person from whom so much has been taken, and partly at Gwen's hands.

"Why did the DSMB make you stressed?"

"The Thursday calls were always about the pediatric cancer trials," she says. "You worry about those ones the most. At least I used to. Before I got fired."

Suki steps aside to let Gwen into the house. Gwen steps inside with her cloth bag, then turns to face her former subject.

"I'm sorry that happened to you—"

"Why are you here?" Suki interrupts, arms folded, looking at the floor and clearly not interested in Gwen's apology.

"I need your help."

"And why in the world would I help *you*?" she says, the corner of her mouth turned up in a tight grin. "I know you were just doing your job and all, but you did play a pretty big part in ruining my life."

"Let's just say it's another hunch," Gwen says. "I think after you hear what I'm going to tell you, you'll want to help me. But if not, I promise I'll leave you alone with no questions asked."

Gwen can't even imagine what it's been like for Suki since the story broke. There's an absence about her that's unmistakable. She looks drained, hollowed out, diminished. Gwen forces herself to maintain eye contact and stay as still as possible, trying to appear earnest and nonthreatening like a hunter to a skittish deer.

After what seems like an eternity, Suki nods and silently leads her into the kitchen.

Her daughter is sitting at their kitchen table, legs tucked underneath her for height as she leans forward and takes a big bite of a grilled cheese sandwich. When they walk in, she glances up from the iPad next to her plate, a look of curiosity on her face as she chews with cheeks puffed out and a drip of orange-yellow cheese on her chin. Suki ignores the silent question and shoos her kid away so that Mom and her friend can have some privacy.

She also doesn't introduce the *friend* to her daughter.

Once the little girl is gone with her sandwich and iPad, Suki swipes the crumbs off the table and offers Gwen a seat.

"Coffee?" she asks, heading over to the pot in the corner of a countertop cluttered with Styrofoam and cardboard takeout containers. Gwen's staring at a stack of pizza boxes on the island when Suki turns to her holding out the pot, raising it and shrugging slightly, silently repeating her offer.

"Oh, yeah, sure. That'd be great," Gwen says, smiling and trying to pretend that she wasn't just in the process of estimating how many meals are represented by the empty containers strewn throughout the kitchen.

"I'm not lazy, you know. I'm just doing my part to support the local economy during these trying times," Suki says, waving her hands at the scene. She fills two mugs, heads over to the table, taking the seat across from Gwen, and sighs. "My husband usually handled the cooking."

"And now?" Gwen asks, taking the offered mug.

"He left me. Us."

The accusation hangs in the air.

Gwen doesn't fight it. She breathes in the aroma of pumpkin

spice, takes a sip, then gives Suki a nod of approval. She points at the arsenal of containers.

"I can relate," she says. "My boyfriend used to do all of the cooking in our relationship too. He was a chef."

"Not anymore?" Suki asks, taking a sip.

"No, he's dead," Gwen says, watching curiosity ripple across Suki's brow at her pronouncement. "Other people are too, which is why I'm here."

SHE DOESN'T HOLD back any details, figuring full disclosure is the best way to gain any semblance of trust, whatever that might look like given their circumstances.

She tells Suki about the election committee's test and Gwen's selection as Rosemary Martin's data miner, the man who came for her at the Watergate, how he murdered Darnell, burned down his restaurant, and then attacked Gwen again at the Harvester research facility, and possibly killed Evelyn. She tells her about getting back online at Oliver's house, getting kicked off the system, and her decision to come to Boston.

She even tells Suki about her dad.

She tells her everything, and by the time she's done, she feels she should be mentally exhausted. But she's not. She's enthralled, amped up, and fascinated—because she's been observing Suki's reactions to her story. She's only known the woman across from her as a series of biological outputs, bits of human information that generated hypotheses, probabilities, and enticing analyses, but now she's witnessing the flesh and blood and bone, the physical human behind the data. How a spike of adrenaline in the bloodstream or an increase in nerve signaling actually *looks* on her subject's face. The slight lift of an eyebrow or clench of her jaw. For Gwen, telling the story is an almost out-of-body experience as she watches Suki, a data golem come to life, her own personal

Frankenstein's monster, sipping coffee across the kitchen table in a bathrobe and slippers.

"It sounds like you're stuck in the middle of some sort of massive cover-up," Suki says. She reaches out and touches the side of the portable array. "But I don't understand what you need from me."

"Miners can only access the system when they're tethered to a subject," Gwen says. "And right now, because the senator's Harvester is somehow disabled, I'm not tethered to anyone." She picks up the tethering ring. "But the last time I was in the system, you were still in my queue, so . . ."

Suki's eyes widen and her eyebrows rise as understanding dawns on her. For a moment she's frozen, then she slams down her mug, a splash of coffee licking over the rim and splattering her sleeve.

"Are you serious?" she says, shooting up from her chair. "Do you really expect me to let you put me back online?"

"Just long enough for me to get back into the system and access my data," Gwen says. "That's it, I promise."

Suki studies her stained sleeve, thumbing the coffee as it absorbs into the terry cloth, then shrugs off the robe. She tosses it onto a chair and paces back and forth in front of the stove. Gwen wants to say more, to assure this woman that no harm will come to her if she's put back into the system, but she stops herself, knowing that any assurances will ring hollow coming from her. Instead, she waits and hopes.

"You shouldn't have come here," Suki says, looking at Gwen over the top of a pile of mail on her kitchen island. "You should go talk to the police. They can protect your father. You have to let *them* deal with this at this point."

"I will," Gwen says, getting up from the table and slowly walking over to Suki. "But these people are hiding something. And it's something bad enough that they're willing to kill to keep it a secret. They disabled the senator's Harvester. They could be trying to erase my data right now, or change it somehow. I have no idea. That's why I have to get back in there quickly, before it's too late."

Suki rubs her Harvester tattoo. She looks like she's about to say something, then stops herself. After a few seconds she starts again, but then seems to realize that she's scratching at her forearm, leaving pinkish streaks across the dull gray swirls and lines of the tattoo. She pulls her pajama sleeve over her forearm and holds the end of it in her fist.

"I can't," she says, her voice breaking. "You don't know how it feels. I'd give anything for this thing to be out of my body. Since the day you exposed my affair, I've dreamed of nothing else. And now you're asking me to let you turn it back on."

"I know. I know what I'm asking. And I wish there was some other way," Gwen says. "But I need to put an end to this. And I think I can, right now. But only if you help me."

Suki looks like she's about to say something when her daughter sneaks around the corner and into the kitchen.

"Mommy, Puffy pooped in the front room again," the girl says. She seems to be working hard to not look at the stranger in her kitchen, but her eyes dart over to Gwen repeatedly.

"I'll come get it in a minute," Suki says, waving her daughter toward her. When the girl gets there, Suki takes her shoulders and faces her toward Gwen. "Sammy, say hi to my friend from work."

Gwen kneels in front of the girl so she's on her level and extends her hand.

"I'm Gwen. It's nice to meet you, Sammy."

"Hi," Sammy says, taking Gwen's outstretched hand and giving it two quick pumps. "Did you get fired too?"

Gwen can feel the blood rushing to her cheeks even as her heart breaks at the girl's question. She looks up at Suki, whose lip is quivering as she strokes the girl's hair.

"No, honey," her mom says. "That was just me. Now go keep Puffy company, okay?"

The girl jogs away and Gwen stands up, but she struggles to meet Suki's gaze.

"I can't imagine how terrible this is for you."

"Can I ask you a question?" Suki says, wiping tears from her cheeks. "Do you ever think about the person?"

"What?"

"The person. Do you ever think about the person you're assigned to?"

"I try to stay as objective as possible, so I focus only on the data coming through the system," Gwen says. This is the same answer she's always given when someone asks her this question. And she's always thought it was a good answer. But today, standing in Suki's kitchen after meeting her little girl, it feels evasive and dumb, and she hates herself for saying the words the second they escape her lips.

"I get that. But even so, you know that what you're looking at on those screens is someone's actual life, right?"

Gwen nods, searching for a response. All her beliefs about the greater good and protecting the public—the beliefs she's formulated and held so tightly for years, the ideology she's clung to since the day they convicted her father and dragged him away to prison—all of it feels broken in this cold, harsh moment, staring into Suki's watery eyes.

"Just now," Suki continues, "you said that you need to get back into the system to save *your* data. But it's not yours, Gwen. It's someone else's. Those data are someone else's *life*."

Gwen suddenly feels defensive. "I'm not the one passing judgment," she says. "That's not my job. I just give people access to the information. *They* decide what matters."

"That's where you're fooling yourself," Suki says. "Because what you're giving people is incomplete. It's only part of the truth."

"Nothing is ever complete," Gwen says. "But this is pretty darn close. Closer than we've ever been able to get before."

"No, Gwen, it's not. You might be able to see inside my blood and know every nuance of it. Know every protein floating around in there, its composition, all my biology's flaws and potential. But you can't see inside my heart or mind." Suki pushes up her sleeve and holds out her Harvester tattoo. "This thing only gives you part of the picture. What I did—"

Her voice catches in her throat, and she takes a moment to collect herself before continuing.

"What I did was terrible, and I'm paying a really high price for it. So is my daughter, and for that, I'll never forgive myself. But this tattoo, and that machine over there on the table, they don't tell you anything about the loneliness and absence of real affection that led to what I did. The years of drifting apart and a relationship that had become purely transactional. And this tattoo can't tell you anything about the sadness and remorse that consumes my life now. All of that is missing from what you see, and all of that is part of me. This miracle of science and technology lets you see inside a person's body, but don't you dare pretend it lets you look into someone's soul."

Guilt weighs on Gwen as she stands in silence, Suki's words hanging around her like fog. Nearby on the kitchen table, the portable array sits like a mini monolith to Gwen's most closely held tenets, which now feel hollow and abstract, irrelevant in the face of Suki's grief.

"You're right," she says. "I know I don't get the whole picture. I know I'm missing . . . a lot," she concedes for the first time since she sat behind an array and watched another human's data stream past her on the screens. "I just . . . I've always hoped that if I got enough of it, maybe I could protect innocent people from getting hurt."

Suki nods and wipes her eyes with her sleeve. "I dedicated my adult life to helping people, so I understand that impulse," she says. "But I'm not helping people now, because my career is over. That's what your tattoo did. What you did. You prevented me from doing my job. And I was really good at it."

"I'm so sorry, Suki. Truly, I am," Gwen says.

Suki leans back against the sink and lets out a deep breath. She folds back her pajama sleeve once more and runs her fingers over her Harvester tattoo, lightly tracing its dull lines and swirls. From the next room, Puffy lets out a flurry of barks, followed by a burst of high-pitched giggling from Sammy. The two women smile at one another, delighting in the happy sounds.

Then Suki walks over and gently rests her hand on Gwen's bandaged shoulder.

"Okay," she says. "I'll do it."

———

GWEN SLIPS the tethering ring over Suki's hand and watches as it contracts. When it's snug against her wrist, the dark metal brightens to a light gray and begins to roll up Suki's forearm and over her tattoo. It climbs up to her elbow, matching her arm's thickness as it goes, then reverses its path back down to her wrist. When it stops, it beeps three times, and a square panel slides open on the top of the ring.

Gwen gets up from the table. "Do you have a sharp knife?"

"Drawer left of the stove," Suki says. "The last time I was tethered to you the person used a whole vial of your blood. You're not going to . . .?"

"No, don't worry. This one only needs a few drops," Gwen says, opening the drawer. She roots around, takes out a small paring knife, and comes back to the table. She pokes the tip of the knife through her thumb hard enough to break the skin, then squeezes her thumb pad until a bead of bright red blood wells to the surface. She holds it over the open panel.

As the first drop hits the ring, the color changes from gray to a soft white.

At the second drop, it brightens more.

When the third drop falls, the panel slides shut and the ring flashes between bright white and red. After a series of beeps, the ring begins its climb up Suki's arm again. As it crawls over her tattoo, the color shifts from white to silver as the tattoo's dormant circuitry comes alive. At Suki's elbow, the ring begins to descend, reactivating the circuitry that tethered them before. It comes to a stop at Suki's wrist, her tattoo once again glowing a soft blue, indicating that the process is complete.

"As terrible as it sounds, I did miss the blue," Suki says as the tethering ring grows and she's able to take it off her wrist. "It's a good nightlight."

Gwen reaches for the portable array, which emits a hum as soon as she touches its surface.

"That's a good sign," she says as she positions it in front of her and rests her palm on the side of the cylinder. The blood draw port slides open and Gwen places her index finger on it. Seconds later, the device projects a keyboard and screen.

Gwen asks Suki for her Wi-Fi password, then taps it onto the tabletop projection of the keyboard. She can tell that Suki is curious to see what happens, this part having always been shielded from her—as it is from all the people of consequence who are monitored. Gwen waves her around to sit next to her as the startup screens flash and the familiar home screen appears.

Suki's icon is now green. Rosemary Martin's is still amber. But when Gwen clicks on Rosemary's icon, the results from her last analysis of the senator's respiratory tract appear on the screen.

Pulmonary analysis complete. Exposure to foreign air pollutants confirmed. Bilateral infiltrates of the subject's lung parenchyma are consistent with inhaled particulate matter 2.5, a common air pollutant found at high levels in several major cities in Asia.

"Is that it?" Suki asks, pointing to the message.

"That's it."

"It says it's common, though."

"Yeah, but I also found high levels of *Hantavirus* antibodies in her system."

"That's weird," Suki says.

"It is. If I can figure out which parts of Asia have high levels of both this particulate matter 2.5 and *Hantavirus*, it should tell me where she's been."

Gwen fingers start to tap away on Suki's kitchen table, and a multitude of windows open on the screen, each filled with dense blocks of text.

"What's all that?"

"I did a search for the most recent environmental impact studies conducted in Asia."

"Shit, there's tons," Suki says as Gwen does a quick scan through the windows. "It'll take forever to dig through those."

Gwen calls up a black window with a blinking green cursor and starts to enter lines of code. "Don't worry, I'm pretty good at my job too," she says as her fingers tap a frantic beat on Suki's tabletop.

"I know," Suki says with a sarcastic tone, but then softens it with a chuckle.

"I'll just run a search algorithm across all of them at once and . . . voila!"

One of the windows pops to the forefront with a line of text highlighted in yellow.

"It looks like there's high levels of particulate matter 2.5 and endemic *Hantavirus* in a densely populated region of . . . holy shit. North Korea?"

"Are you sure?"

"*This* is what they're trying to hide. It has to be," Gwen says, her fingers hovering over the laser keyboard, hands shaking too much to type.

They both stare at the screen silently.

"This is a pretty massive thing to even suggest," Suki eventually says, letting her hand drift over her tattoo. "A presidential candidate connected to North Korea? I mean, think of the shit storm that'll happen when this gets out. What if you're wrong?"

Gwen clenches her fists repeatedly, her knuckles cracking with each squeeze as she considers the implications. But then she thinks of Darnell and Evelyn and her father . . . and her resolve returns.

She sets her fingers on the glowing keyboard. "I'm not wrong," she says.

She starts to type, and new windows appear on the screen.

"Social media?" Suki says.

"People need to see this. And since the senator is offline, I'm prevented from broadcasting through the Harvester. So I'll just have to put it out there the old-fashioned way."

Gwen pastes the respiratory analysis results on multiple social media sites, adds a bunch of hashtags for Harvester watchdog sites, and posts the info.

"That should get people talking."

And it does.

Reactions to the posts start coming in almost immediately, a few comments at first and then a flood only minutes later. As the public response grows, Gwen sits back in her seat and offers Suki her hand.

"What do we do now?" Suki asks, taking Gwen's hand.

"We watch."

CLAUDIA STEPS off the elevator and walks to the front desk, trying to calm her frayed nerves by using the breathing exercises her therapist taught her. But it's too quiet in the hospital and the eeriness breaks her concentration. Since her boss was brought in, the hospital staff have been sending all other emergency room patients to neighboring hospitals, so the only people in the lobby are a couple of nurses, an EMS worker, and a few police officers.

"I'm sorry, ma'am. This area is closed."

Claudia turns toward the young woman in light blue scrubs approaching her, but an officer waves the woman off before Claudia can respond.

"It's okay," the officer says. "This is the senator's chief of staff."

Claudia nods to the apologetic young nurse then turns to the police sergeant, who she recalls is one of the people who responded to Rosemary's 911 call.

"How's the senator?" he asks.

"She's resting," Claudia says. "Luckily the cut on her arm wasn't too deep, so she doesn't need surgery. Any updates on the search?"

"Detectives are still canvassing the scene. Secret Service is there too," he says. "The county coroner just left with the senator's driver. We haven't gotten to his next of kin yet, so please make sure your office keeps his identity under wraps."

"Thanks," she says, heading for the front doors. "I'll have someone from our press office coordinate with the sheriff's office."

"Sure thing," he says, keeping stride with her. "Listen, there's quite a crowd out there. Do you want me to have someone escort you out?"

"Shit, really?" Claudia quickens her pace toward the two officers flanking the front entrance. When she reaches them, she sees a large group of people gathered under the portico. Her hopes of getting back to campaign headquarters unmolested by the press are thoroughly dashed. She checks her watch, then turns to the sergeant. "Thank you, an escort would be great."

"Everyone's on crowd control, Sarge," one of the officers by the doors says, shaking her head in disbelief. "It's a zoo out there."

"I'll take you out myself," the sergeant says to Claudia. "Stay close to me."

Claudia pauses. "It might help if I take a few questions from the press first, just to calm everyone down."

"You sure about that?" he asks.

"Just a couple," she says, tucking a stray strand of hair behind her ear. "It'll be fine. Let's go."

As the heavy glass doors slide open, a wave of sound crashes into the hospital lobby. Lights atop cameras flare to life as Claudia and the police sergeant step into the fray. Dozens of people are shouting her name as she shields her eyes from the intense light. She knows they're asking about the attack on the senator, but their voices blend into an incoherent soup of nouns and verbs without discernable substance.

She walks a few steps and stops, grabbing hold of the sergeant's sleeve. He puts his arms out wide and yells for the crowd to quiet down.

It doesn't work.

She holds up one hand to the crowd, hoping it'll get their attention. But everyone keeps shouting at her, trying to outdo their neighbors. She hasn't been this inundated since the day they announced Rosemary's candidacy.

Once her eyes adjust, she sees several familiar faces from their daily press gaggles. She points to a reporter who interviewed her last month on the campaign trail and shouts to him.

"Mike, go ahead," she says.

"What's the senator's condition?" Mike yells over competing questions from the others.

Claudia waves her arm side to side, karate chopping the air and hoping it'll cut off the shouts. When the noise goes down a few decibels, she yells back to the reporter.

"Senator Martin sustained a laceration on her forearm during the attack but is otherwise fine. She's resting comfortably and anticipates being back on the campaign trail in the coming days."

"There's reports that her driver was killed. Can you confirm?" someone shouts from the side.

"Unfortunately, yes. But that is all I can say at this time."

The fervor from the reporters intensifies now that there's literal blood in the metaphoric waters. "Do you have any leads on the attacker?" another reporter shouts. "Has anyone claimed responsibility?"

"I can't comment—"

"Do you suspect terrorism?"

"What was Senator Martin doing out at that hour?"

"Is there a connection to the attack on the Watergate?"

"Her Harvester's offline. Was it damaged in the attack?

"As I was saying," Claudia shouts, raising both hands to try and quell the onslaught. The sergeant takes a few steps toward the crowd and yells for everyone to calm down, which helps to silence enough people that Claudia can speak without yelling at the top of her lungs.

"I can't comment on the investigation at this time. Multiple agencies are working as we speak, and we hope to have more information in the coming hours. There will be a full briefing later this morning at our campaign headquarters."

But the crowd isn't satisfied, and a swirl of new questions comes at Claudia from all quarters.

The sergeant leans in close to her. "We gotta get you out of here."

"Yeah, I'm done. Let's go," she says.

"All right, make a path!" he yells at the crowd.

But his voice sounds unnecessarily loud, because a sudden quiet has overcome the press of reporters. Suddenly no one's paying attention to either him or to Claudia. They're all engrossed in their phones.

Claudia's confused as she watches people nudge one another and compare screens. Several reporters at the front are swiping and typing with occasional glances at her. Finally, the crowd's collective gaze settles on her, and the silence shatters in an eruption of voices.

None of them are friendly.

"Claudia, what can you tell us about the senator's connection to North Korea?" Mike shouts, his cameraman adjusting his lens as he's knocked around by others pushing in.

Claudia thinks she's misheard. She cups her hand to one ear.

"What is Senator Martin's relationship with North Korea?" he repeats.

"I don't know what you're talking about, Mike," Claudia says, surprised by the out-of-left-field nature of the question. She can feel her own phone vibrating in her jacket pocket and is desperate to grab it and see what's riled everyone up, but there's no need. Another reporter lets her know.

"Numerous sources are reporting on evidence that shows Senator Martin has spent a significant amount of time in North Korea," the reporter shouts, reading from her phone. The others let her continue, pushing their microphones forward. "Yet there's no record of Rosemary Martin ever having been to North Korea or having any reason to go there. Can you comment?"

"I'm afraid I'm not sure where people are getting this information," Claudia begins, "but I assure you—"

The same reporter interrupts. "The information comes from Harvester, though rather than being broadcast from the system, it was shared on social media sites. That said, both the Associated Press and Reuters have confirmed it as authentic."

Claudia looks around at the eager faces before her, microphones thrust out and camera lenses trained on her. She's sure they can see her grasping for a response, her head swirling at the news—information that she was unaware of and yet, somewhere in the back of her mind and depths of her heart, she senses is true.

I've been with her for almost a decade, she thinks as sweat breaks out across her back despite the early morning chill. She feels her face flush and begins to suspect what will be confirmed later that night when she watches herself on all the broadcasts on every channel.

She's helpless—and she looks it.

"I'm sorry," she says. "The senator—" she sputters, then shifts to, "I have no comments at this time."

And that's when the attack hounds break their chains and go for the jugular.

"What are you hiding?" shouts a reporter.

"Senators on both sides of the aisle are calling for an investigation. Will Senator Martin comply?"

"Was this 'accident,' and the convenient destruction of the senator's Harvester, a plot to hide information from the American people?"

Claudia shields her face as she and the sergeant try several avenues to get through the crowd. But the press surges toward them, closing them in on all sides. Eventually the sergeant grabs Claudia's arm and drags her back toward the hospital, where his two officers are waiting to stop the crowd from following. He shoves aside a cameraman who steps in their path and gets her back through the doors as the questions continue to fall on them like rocks from bullies.

Inside the lobby, Claudia breaks away from everyone to be alone. *Breathe*, she thinks. *Just breathe*. Her phone vibrates again, but she ignores it as she looks around the lobby and realizes . . .

Everyone is looking at her.

Her phone's vibrations are insistent. She fishes it out of her pocket and sees that it's the Speaker of the House.

"Mister Speaker," she says, pressing the phone tightly to her ear to keep herself from dropping it. Her hand quivers as she listens to a barrage of commands. After the brief deluge, the line goes dead, and she puts the phone back into her pocket.

The sergeant waits a few seconds before coming over to her.

"Is everything okay?"

"No," she says, with a chuckle that comes from deep in her chest. "In fact, I'd say everything is pretty good and fucked."

"We have a few cars on the way. My team's gonna clear the press from the front of the hospital. Then we can get you where you need to go."

She looks at him and nods, but instead of waiting, she turns around and heads back to the elevators.

"Where are you going?" he asks.

"I need to talk to my boss. I have some questions for her."

We continue to follow a developing story swirling around Senator Rosemary Martin. For those of you just joining us, information emerged earlier today suggesting that Senator Martin, the Republican presidential candidate—and before today, a double-digit favorite heading into November—was exposed at some point in the past to certain air pollutants found primarily in North Korea. People from around the world have been poring over old Harvester data analyses, records of the senator's official business abroad, and other publicly available information, with a singular question: What is the connection between Senator Martin and the communist regime in North Korea?

So far, the Martin camp has not released a statement about these findings, nor have they commented on an alleged connection to the attacks on the Watergate or a mysterious crash that led to the death of a high-placed government official involved in the management of data mining personnel. For more on this story, we turn to Xander with our Washington affiliate—

"It's your turn," Sammy says.

Gwen looks away from the television and back to the gameboard. She takes the top card from the pile, finds a single blue square, and reaches for her gingerbread character. But before she can move her game piece, Sammy does it for her.

"Oh no, you're lost in the lollipops. You wanna pick a better card?"

"No, that's okay," Gwen says.

"But you lose your next turn," the girl says, arms out wide to accentuate the dramatic turn of events.

"That's okay, honey," Suki says, reaching for the stack of cards. "Gwen likes playing by the rules."

Gwen smiles at Suki, who is happily showing off her newly drawn card with double red squares. "Nice one."

"Looks like things are getting interesting for the senator," Suki says as she jumps her gingerbread figure along the candy path.

"People are starting to connect the dots," Gwen replies. "The truth will eventually come out, whatever it is."

"What are *you* going to do?" Suki asks.

"I imagine I'll be spending a million hours answering questions."

"No, I mean afterwards. What will you do next?"

"After all that's happened . . . I honestly don't know," Gwen says, giving Sammy a thumbs-up on her double purple square card. *If only it were as easy as just picking up the next card*, she thinks as the little girl with the big smile slowly slides her gingerbread token across the board toward the finish line.

Gwen reaches for the draw pile but is stopped short by Sammy, who waggles her index finger at her to remind her that her turn is skipped, then jumps up and dashes into the kitchen, suddenly in need of a treat.

"How about you?" Gwen asks now that Sammy is out of earshot. "Any chance you and your husband might work things out?"

"I don't think so," Suki says as she takes a card and moves her piece.

"I'm sorry, I don't mean to pry."

"It's fine," Suki says with a sad smile. "I think once we sell this place and get settled somewhere new, I'll probably go back into medicine. Practice pediatrics again someplace quiet and focus on Sammy."

"I'm glad to hear that."

Sammy walks back toward them with a plate piled high with Oreos. A few cookies break loose from the pile and drop to the carpet, and Sammy pauses to chase down the runaways.

A knock comes from the front door. Suki and Gwen exchange a glance, then Suki goes to answer it.

"Hello, Mrs. Hammamoto," the man at the door says. "My name is Joe Quincy. I'm here for Gwen."

Gwen stands up as Suki invites him inside.

"What gives, Quincy?" Gwen says from across the room. "You're not wearing your disguise."

"Excuse me?" he says, standing just inside the door, a confused look on his face.

"Where's your baseball cap?" Gwen walks over and shakes his hand. "Not very covert."

"Right," he says with a smile. "I'm glad you're okay, Ms. Elliott."

"Did you talk to the prison?"

"I spoke with the warden, and she agreed to have your father moved to solitary until we can ascertain the threat against him. I also talked to Secret Service, and they're going to dispatch personnel to join the guard detail on your father's level. He's safe."

Gwen's sigh catches in her throat.

"We need to get you back to Washington," Quincy continues. "There's an army of people looking to talk to you."

"Just a sec," she says.

She walks back over to Sammy, who's sitting cross-legged by the gameboard.

"You're leaving?" the girl asks, her lips ringed in black cookie dust.

"I'm sorry I can't finish the game," Gwen says, holding out her hand. "But it was really nice meeting you."

Sammy gives her the same two-pump shake as earlier. "Maybe we can play another time?"

"I'd like that."

When Gwen goes back to the door, Suki is waiting with Oliver's cloth bag containing the portable array and tethering ring. She hands it to Gwen, who in turn hands it over to Quincy.

Gwen meets Suki's gaze. Suddenly she feels awkward. "I don't know what to say."

"You're welcome," Suki says, then gives Gwen a quick hug.

"I wish . . ." Gwen starts, but then shifts to what she really wants to tell her. "I thought I knew you, and I'm really glad I was wrong."

As they drive away, Suki and Sammy are standing in the door, waving goodbye. Gwen waves back and keeps watch until they turn off Suki's street.

"It must have been weird meeting her face to face," Quincy says.

"It was," Gwen agrees. "But I think it was also really important. For both of us."

A STEADY STREAM of people joins the protesters behind sawhorses and ribbons of yellow police tape. Officers in riot gear hold the line near the hospital entrance, where several black SUVs sit idling. Chants go up here and there and are quickly echoed by most of the crowd. Some wave homemade signs taped to sticks and two-by-fours, while others pump their fists and stomp their feet. A few in the crowd stab the sky with lit tiki torches on long bamboo poles. At the edges of the assembly, camera lights flicker on and off in the gloaming as reporters give updates to their viewers at home.

All that's missing are a few pitchforks and a stake, Spencer thinks as he glares down at them from an open window and swipes through photos of Rosemary on his phone.

At the diner in Ohio where she officially kicked off her campaign.

Holding a *Martin for President* sign and giving the camera a thumbs-up.

Asleep next to him in a hotel bed, hair tousled over a bare shoulder.

He zooms in on her face. She looks so peaceful, so content. *This is the only time she's ever still*, he thinks, tracing her jawline with his thumb, just like he did that night, remembering the smoothness of her skin.

Leaving hospital. Where are you?

He swipes the notification off the screen, but it's too late. The spell is broken.

He sets the phone aside and stares at the scene below. Little pops of light burst amid the crowd as people pose for selfies or group photos. He imagines the hashtags decorating the images of the righteous.

#FuckMartin

#KoreaGate

#Truth

What he wouldn't give to go down there. Burn their signs and knock the teeth out of loudmouths. Thrash and stomp and stab all the "truth-seekers" who walked here from their million-dollar homes or drove here in their imported luxury cars. Show them the *real* truth of their pampered, selfish, obnoxious, fat lives. How dare they demand truth while hiding from it under silk sheets and gilded stories told to them by their parents and their parents' parents about an American dream achievable by only a precious, protected few?

These people have no idea what is true in this world. What I wouldn't give to show them.

Down below, the hospital's front doors slide open and several officers emerge. Rosemary's entourage follows closely behind, scurrying to a waiting SUV as an avalanche of vitriol washes over them, the noise from the penned-in crowd exploding as the guilty try to make their escape.

That's when he sees her.

She's flanked by her chief of staff and press secretary, each with a hand on her, guiding her forward. Her injured arm is in a sling and she's moving tentatively, watching the chaos swirl around her. The crowd howls its outrage as the police work to keep everyone in check and away from their prey.

She takes in the scene around her.

She looks pale.

Weak.

Frightened.

From this distance, it should be impossible to see these things clearly. But through the scope of his rifle, he can tell with absolute certainty . . . she's afraid.

He knows her face so well.

And he knows she isn't afraid of the people there to revel in her downfall, to curse and condemn her. No, she's beyond that now. She's afraid of something else.

She's afraid of him.

Of what he'll do. What he must do.

He settles the crosshair on her forehead.

Goodbye, my love, he whispers.

And pulls the trigger.

CHAPTER
TWENTY-NINE

Two months later

GWEN WALKS through the metal detector and waits for her stuff to reach her at the end of the belt. The security officer spends a few extra seconds examining the scan of her backpack before sending everything along.

"Looks good," he says.

"Can you really tell?"

"Nah, but all I had today was a granola bar from the vending machine, so even black-and-white mystery food looks good to me," he says with a chuckle.

She takes her boots and jacket out of the gray plastic tub, lifts her bag from the belt, and carries everything to a nearby chair to get situated.

As she pulls on her boots, the warden enters the room and walks over to her.

"Ms. Elliot, everything is set," she says. "We cleared the yard, so it'll just be the two of you."

"Thank you," Gwen says. "Do you have any updates on timing?"

"The Justice Department said we'll know something for sure by the end of this week. But I don't expect any problems with the transfer request."

Gwen picks up her bag, stands, and shakes the warden's hand. "Thanks for all you've done to keep him safe."

"It was my pleasure." She opens the door that leads to the recreation area. "It's the least we could do after all you did to keep this country safe."

Gwen gives her a slight nod, then heads outside. Her involvement in what happened with Rosemary Martin is not widely known—to protect her from any sort of retaliation—and it makes her uncomfortable when the few who do know lavish any sort of attention on her, or mistakenly suggest that what she did was driven by some sort of deep-seated patriotism. It wasn't. She did it to protect her dad. And, if she's being honest with herself, she did it because she had to know. She had to finish the puzzle.

If she's being *really* honest with herself, she'll admit that she did it for revenge, too.

Her dad is in all orange, as usual, but is also wearing a puffy blue winter coat, one that's too thick and too protective for the slight chill in the air. His cheeks and nose have a pink hue to them as he stands up and waits for her at the table, blowing air into his cupped hands to warm them.

"I'm warning you," he says, taking her in his arms and giving her a hug. "Ten weeks in a row. I'm getting used to this."

She sits down and sets her backpack on the table. He grabs it, unzips the main compartment, and starts taking out the Tupperware containers inside.

"What have we got?"

"Turkey, stuffing—just the boxed kind, nothing fancy—some of those sweet potatoes you like, and cranberry sauce," Gwen says. "I used a heating pack in the bag, but it still might have gotten a little cold."

He pops open the first big container with the turkey and stuffing and takes a sniff.

"You make the bird?"

"First one ever," she says. "I'm still getting used to the whole cooking thing. But I think it came out pretty good."

He takes a bite and nods in agreement. "It's great, honey. Happy Thanksgiving."

As he scoops some of the stuffing into his mouth, she notes his sharp cheekbones and hopes the food helps put some meat on his frame.

"So," she says. "It sounds like your transfer is gonna happen any day now. The warden told me they should get the official word soon."

"That's great to hear." He digs through the backpack and pulls out a few paper packets of salt and pepper. "It's crazy, but I miss the noise. I used to hate it the first few years. There's no such thing as *quiet* in this place. But after more than two months in solitary, I'm looking forward to the soundtrack again."

She looks at him sideways. "Soundtrack?"

"That's what we lifers call the background noise. You know, like those old-time radio stations that play 'the soundtrack of your life'?"

"And a guy farting a few cells over is your soundtrack?"

"Right now," he says, pointing back at the prison with his spork, "that'd be music to my ears."

This is the third or fourth time he's brought up the isolation, and she's worried it's really getting to him.

"I am sorry about all this," Gwen says. "They still don't have any leads on the people who came after me or the ones involved in Senator Martin's assassination, and of course, North Korea is still denying any involvement, so for now they're just being really super cautious. I know it sucks."

She can tell he's trying to set her mind at ease as he waves it off and scoops up some of the deep-red, jellied cranberries. She watches him chew, then realizes she forgot something. She pulls the bag toward her, unzips the front pocket, and pulls out a Ziploc filled with buttery croissants. Her dad's eyes light up as she hands him one and then takes one for herself.

"Can I ask you something?" he says after savoring a big bite of the roll dipped in congealed brown gravy.

"Of course."

"I'm nervous to ask because I don't want you to get mad at me. And it'd kill me if it made you stop coming. But all I've got is time on my hands to think these days and I can't stop wondering about something."

"It's okay, Dad," she says, resting her hand on his arm. "What's up?"

"Seriously, it's been so nice seeing you every week. I can't tell you what it means to me."

"I'm glad," she says, sensing what's coming next, knowing her dad hates unanswered questions as much as she does.

"But I'm curious, honey . . . what changed?"

"Between us, you mean?"

"I know you went through a really traumatic experience. I can't even imagine what it was like. And it's probably got you re-evaluating a lot of things."

"It has," she says, putting down the roll and brushing greasy crumbs off her hands.

"And look, like I said, I'm not complaining," he says, reaching out and taking her hand. "But I can't help but think there's got to be more to it."

She squeezes his thin hand and looks across the table at him. For so long, she couldn't bear the sight of him. But now, seeing him here eating a meal she made for him, she regrets all the lost time.

"What were your hole cards?" she says.

"What? Hole cards?"

"The day they came for you, we were playing poker with Harry and the gang. I had pocket deuces and the table showed ace, deuce, deuce, king, ace. I was all in with that four of a kind, but we never finished."

He smiles at her and raps his knuckles on the table. "I can't believe you've been thinking about that hand all this time."

"You know me," she says. "I couldn't wait to turn those deuces over and sweep in all your chips. It was gonna be amazing. But then the cops busted in."

She watches as his smile disappears and the corner of his mouth quivers. He tries to hide it but fails.

"I'll never forgive myself for putting you through that," he says.

"Did you have 'em?" she asks. "And don't lie. I'll know."

He pauses, his eyes filling with tears, then nods. "Yeah, I had the aces. I'm sorry."

A broad smile breaks out on her face and a sense of calm washes over her body, making her feel lighter than she's felt in years.

"That's fantastic!" she says too loudly, then quickly glances around the prison yard, happy they're alone. "Really, I'm so glad. You have no idea."

Confusion is etched across her father's wrinkled forehead. "I don't understand."

Gwen lets out a quick laugh to let him know that it's okay, which seems to just confuse him more.

"Dad, I've never been surer about anything in my life than that poker hand. And now, all these years later, to find out I was wrong? It's like . . . freedom."

He still looks confused, so she leans forward across the table and kisses him on both of his moist cheeks, thumbing away the stray tears when she's done.

"I'll never understand why you did what you did, Dad. And that's okay, because I'm finally willing to not let that mistake be all that you are to me. You're more than that and always have been. I understand that now. And that's what's changed."

Her dad gets up from the table, comes around, and collapses into her, hugging her as deep sobs rack his thin frame. She hugs him back, truly, for the first time since before his arrest.

After a few minutes he lets her go, but he stays next to her at the table, holding her hands.

"So what's next?" he says.

"First, we get you situated. The new prison is a little further away, but I should still be able to visit you a lot. We'll work it out, I promise."

He nods, but quickly shifts the focus to her. "For you, I mean. What's next for you?"

She reaches for the Tupperware container of turkey and stuffing and hands it to her dad, making him take another bite before answering.

"Well, they've offered me my boss's old job, but I don't know. I've spent so much time focused on other people's lives . . . I figure maybe I should spend a little time focusing on my own."

His smile is big and bright.

"I think that sounds like a good idea," he says, kissing her on the top of her head like he used to when she was little. "What will you do first?"

"I don't know yet," she says. "Maybe Vegas."

THE END

ACKNOWLEDGMENTS

Thanks to the pandemic, it was easy to conjure feelings of anxiety, tension, and dread while writing this book. The struggle was finding any sort of lightness or joy that could serve as a counter-balance. Luckily, I had a few reliable sources I could turn to:

My family, who may not understand what I do or why, but who have always supported and believed in me;

My children, whose very existence means I've done something worthwhile and magical in this life;

My wife, who inspires and encourages me to be a better, kinder man;

My D&D crew, who help keep me young—and have done so for decades;

My poker crew, who've never left me "behind" as the seasons rolled on by;

My colleagues and students, who always inspire me to see things in new and different ways;

The Lofi Girl community, who provided the soundtrack for this book and all future books;

And last but by no conceivable means least, my amazing editor, David Gatewood, who makes everything better.

ABOUT THE AUTHOR

Lou Iovino was born in Philadelphia, Pennsylvania. He splits his time between working in advertising, writing, and teaching. He lives in New Jersey with his wife and two sons.

For more information, visit www.louiovino.com. You can also find him on the following social channels:

DATA MINE

LOU IOVINO